. . . When Toni opened her eyes she saw a strange room bright with light. She lay in space touching nothing. Then she turned slightly, finding herself, and her ankles moved against Morgen's. In sleep they had drawn apart all but their ankles. She turned her head and saw Morgen's hair on the pillow and she saw her face, pale with soft fringed shadows under the eyes, her long curved throat. She held her breath. She wanted to melt and pour herself around Morgen like wax.

And when Morgen opened her eyes they clouded with a startled darkness at first and then Toni smiled and said, Don't look at me like that. It makes me feel like an impostor, and then Morgen too smiled and they looked at each other and went back into the night and brought the two they were into the bright tender quietness of the morning.

TORCHLIGHT
TO
VALHALLA

TORCHLIGHT
TO
VALHALLA

a novel by

GALE WILHELM

The Naiad Press Inc.

1985

Printed in the United States of America
First Naiad Press Edition 1985

Typeset by Sandi Stancil
Cover design by Tee A. Corinne

ISBN 0-930044-68-1

WORKS BY GALE WILHELM

Claudia Marseille
Photographer

GALE WILHELM WRITES

In 1934, while I was living in Berkeley, California, I had a short story published in the April issue of LITERARY AMERICA. I think this was my first published short story. There were other stories published in LITERARY AMERICA during 1934 and 1935. LITERARY AMERICA was a monthly magazine published by The Galleon Press in New York City and edited by Kenneth Houston.

In 1934 I submitted the manuscript of WE TOO ARE DRIFTING to Random House and in October of that year Random House refused publication and returned the manuscript. During that year I corresponded with Kenneth Houston and he put me in touch with Frances Pindyck of Pinker and Morrison, Agents, in New York City. Miss Pindyck then submitted WE TOO ARE DRIFTING to Random House. It was accepted by them for publication and was published in the fall of 1935.

In the meantime, also in 1935, Kenneth Houston offered me employment as Associate Editor of LITERARY AMERICA. I accepted his offer and moved to New York City where I lived for a year.

Random House also published my second novel NO LETTERS FOR THE DEAD and my third novel TORCHLIGHT TO VALHALLA. The typescript of

TORCHLIGHT is now at The Bancroft Library of the University of California, along with material requested by them.

My next three novels BRING HOME THE BRIDE, THE TIME BETWEEN and NEVER LET ME GO were published by William Morrow and Company.

As you wrote in your introduction to WE TOO ARE DRIFTING, I was born April 26, 1908, in Eugene Oregon to Ethel Gale Brewer and Wilson Price Wilhelm and was educated in Oregon, Idaho and Washington. I came to the Bay Area in California in my late teens and lived there until I moved to New York City in 1935. I lived for a year in New York, returning to the Bay Area in 1936.

In 1938 I moved to Oakdale, California, and lived there until 1948, when I returned again to the Bay Area. I have lived in Berkeley since 1948 and continuously in my present house for the past 32 years.

Gale Wilhelm
July, 1985

INTRODUCTION

In October, 1984 I completed the introduction to WE TOO ARE DRIFTING. Since that time literally thousands of women have read of our search for the whereabouts of Gale Wilhelm. My lover and partner in Naiad Press, Donna J. McBride, and I had planned to search for her on the west coast in conjunction with our Summer, 1985 trip to ABA and National Women's Studies Association meetings.

In April, 1985, Pat Shannon, her hands visibly trembling, brought a letter addressed to me, Barbara Grier, in care of Naiad Press. Routinely opened in the mail, the innocuous small white envelope, postmarked Toledo, Ohio and without a return address contained a library type p-slip on which was neatly printed the name Gale Wilhelm and a Berkeley, California address and a simple explanation:

(In case you are still
looking for her.)

A Friend

As I had so often done, routinely, in the past, I tried to run the name Gale Wilhelm through long distance telephone information, to learn as I already knew to be true, that no such name was listed in Berkeley. Telephoning my good friend Eric Garber, I gave him the address and asked him to run it through the City Directory and Criss Cross. It turned out that the last time a City Directory was done for Berkeley was in the 1940s but the Criss Cross paid off. There was a listing for that address, the name of another woman, and a telephone number. Ironically, one digit of that number was wrong, to give me another heart-stopping moment when I got a "not is service" response. But checking that "other" name through long distance information quickly showed the one digit printing error and a few moments later I was listening to the telephone ringing in Berkeley.

We had found her. I asked to speak to her, and learned she had just been released from the hospital following treatment for a broken hip, was still on crutches and could not yet be spoken to on the telephone. But the joyous part was started. I was able to explain, through Gale's friend, about the republication of WE TOO ARE DRIFTING, to send her copies of the book, all her reviews and notices, the various articles about her and the book. We tried to convey to her by mail that she had been the object of an intense search (she was later to tell me that she did not consider herself lost for as she put it "I always knew where I was").

In June, 1985, during our summer trips, we were privileged to spend about an hour and a half with Gale and her friend, in their home which replicates the last "rumor" about her whereabouts which was bandied about during the middle 1960s. The rumor went that Gale Wilhelm lived somewhere in the hills above the bay and could see San Francisco from her windows. It's true, she can and no doubt does, daily.

Not well, having had a series of physical ailments including cataract surgery on both eyes, she is still very pleased about the reissuing of her books and the fact that she has a strong present-day following for her work.

As you can see, she provided us with contemporary pictures, and the biographical sketch which follows.

Barbara Grier
August, 1985

TORCHLIGHT TO VALHALLA

SHE was ahead and didn't see him hesitate and almost fall, but she heard the gasp he drew out of the pressing air and, turning, saw his uncertainty, the look of pain and wonder in his face. She started back down the path toward him but he shook his head, standing quite still, and gradually the flush left his face, and breathing cautiously, as though he had been warned within against drawing breath, he said, It's all right, Morgen. We'll go as far as those trees.

She saw them above where the path turned and knew they would spread great soft blankets of shade and she waited and he came up to her slowly, breathing cautiously but smiling to reassure her.

She took his hand. Fritz, she said.

It's all right now, he said.

She pushed back her hair with her free hand and felt her palm damp. We climbed too fast, she said.

He nodded and they went slowly up the little rise to the clump of liveoaks and he sat down and then lay back, folding his arms under his head and stretching out his long thin legs. There, he said. He breathed with difficulty but the cool shaded air lay soft as spray on his face. He felt the blood going outward from his heart again. Somewhere a horse neighed. Morgen put the rucksack down and knelt beside him in the grass. He smiled and then closed his lids over the aching heat in his eyes.

The horse neighed again and Morgen looked out across the canyon toward the sound and then lay back in the grass beside Fritz. Her heart beat heavily. She listened to her heart and to the small whisper of leaves overhead and held the impulse of tears away from her eyes. And Fritz beside her thought, The year has turned past the day again and she is one year older. I am an old man in a crowd watching a child on a carousel. It goes too fast.

They lay like this for a long time and then finally he opened his eyes and lifted himself carefully as though he were brittle. He turned on his side toward Morgen and said, I've lost my appetite but a little beer would be good.

She sat up and got the vacuum bottle out of the rucksack and poured a cup of beer for him and one for herself. He drank lightly and she drank and got out a sandwich made of rye bread and onions in slices so thin they lay like cobwebs on the pink liverwurst. She ate slowly without tasting. Fritz finished his beer and put his pipe unlighted between his teeth.

They were frightened, Morgen because she knew it only as a word in Dr. Stauber's mouth and didn't understand it, Fritz because it had happened again so soon, but they looked out of this fright and away from it out across the canyon with their cool identically blue eyes.

SHE went into the bedroom and sat on the edge of the bed and held her light thin hand on his forehead for a moment. It's cooler, she said. Do you think you can sleep now?

I think so, he said.

She bent and kissed his lips and forehead and hot tired eyes. Good night, Fritz.

He lay looking at her. As though he were continuing a conversation he said, I remember that picture of you best. It was the summer I had to go up to Sacramento. You remember? Morgen nodded and his voice went backward into a shadowed room, and he said, I remember looking and looking at you and wanting to ask God how you'd happened to be. You'd got so tall and you'd forgotten how to smile but your eyes were skies and there was a star in each. That hasn't changed. People will always wonder what it is your eyes hold behind the stars. His own eyes closed and Morgen sat breathing lightly until he stirred and said, If you're wise, my darling, you'll never let them know.

She kissed him again and tucked the covers around his thin shoulders and stood up. She turned out the lamp beside the bed and went back into the studio, leaving his door ajar. She was lost. She thought, If it should happen this time I'd die too, and she went about emptying ashtrays and straightening cushions. She took the coffeepot and cups out into the kitchen and came back quickly and stood before the hearth listening and pulling the fine soft cuffs of her sweater down over her thin wrists. Isolde came quietly from sleep on the windowledge and arched herself against her bare legs. Morgen looked down at her and then sat on the hearth and lifted her up onto her knees. She held her hands close along Isolde's sides and tried to think away from her fear but she thought, He's old. We walked too fast and the sun was too hot on his head, but I must remember, I mustn't let myself forget now that he's old.

She looked down at Isolde and began to stroke her, straight along her back to the tip of her tail. Today for the first time she looked at Fritz and saw an old man.

SHE went slowly around the corner of the house, her arms crossed and her hands held close under her armpits for warmth. In the shadow of the house the air was still very cold. She saw Isolde stalking a leaf on the terrace, ears pointed, belly flattened, her tail quivering at the tip, her hind feet making soft nervous twitches. Then she sprang, incredibly swift and golden and beautiful. Morgen went nearer. Isolde bit at the leaf, rolling over on herself, back and forth along the edge of the terrace. When she heard her name she looked up at Morgen, pretending long thoughtful surprise. Morgen smiled and bent to stroke her but Isolde bit at her thumb and Morgen smiled again and said, All right, I know you're hungry but that isn't the way to get it, and she lifted her and went quietly up the veranda steps to look in at Fritz's window. Morgen saw him sleeping on his back with one arm folded under his head. His body looked slight under the covers and slightly concave.

Above her the wind made small metallic sounds in the eucalyptus tree. A long way off a boat whistled. The sound vibrated softly and deeply on the air and died. Morgen looked out across the bay and saw San Francisco standing like a toy city of shining towers and hills.

Suddenly, without moving, she felt Fritz stir and then the morning stirred around her and she took a swift deep breath of it and turned smiling to the window again.

HE moved and opened his eyes and heard a fly buzzing a noisy monologue in the window and then the room swam upward away from him and settled again but it wasn't the room, it was winter in Vienna, the snow falling and he walking backward to look at his small dark footprints in the snow, the snow falling like many white unhurried butterflies in the evening air.

His eyes had closed and he opened them again, annoyed at himself. He reached toward the table for his pipe and his hand knocked something to the floor, and turning on his side to look for it he saw Morgen smiling at him through the window and Isolde waving the long golden plume of her tail. He lifted his hand gaily and said, Good morning, and yawned like an animal, very openly and heartily.

How are you feeling? Morgen said.

He said, Fine, and felt the cold bowl of his pipe like a little skull in his hand. I'm getting up.

I'll make the coffee then, Morgen said, and went off down the steps and out of his sight.

He lay for a while looking at the place in the air she had occupied, a place thin as a brush handle but lovelier with the still bright look of morning than the morning itself. He rubbed the bowl of the cold pipe along the bridge of his nose. There was a chorus of birds in the acacias and in the air a clean sweet smell of leaves and grass. The day had a singing freshness with no fog to blur it. Morgen liked fog, she liked to walk on the hills when it swept up around her like smoke, and she liked to watch it press against the skylight and curtain the windows at evening; she loved that feeling of being closed in, but she was always happier when a morning came clear and bright out of night.

He hadn't felt finer than this for a long time. He turned back the covers, humming tunelessly to himself, and swung his legs over the edge of the bed and stood up, giving his weight slowly to his long bony feet. His heart made no murmur of protest.

I'M going to take the trowel up to Mark's, she said. The ferrule's loose.

Fritz nodded, absorbed in the first of the three pipes he was allowed for the day. A cloud of smoke drifted up around his head and drifted off. His hair and beard were damp and carefully combed, and there was no shadow of yesterday's pain in his face.

Morgen put the trowel on the veranda railing and pushed her hair back away from her ears. You ought to paint yourself just as you are this morning, Fritz.

He looked at her, little creases forming at the corners of his blue eyes. Maybe I'll do that, he said, when there's nothing else to paint. I'd have to be too old to care particularly what I did. He straightened away from the warm touch of the house against his shoulders. I've a better idea.

What?

You'll know soon enough. By the way, Lubansky's coming up this afternoon. He wants a look at the Chinese album.

She lifted herself up onto the railing and sat beside the trowel. You're not going to let him have it.

Certainly not. He cleared his throat and spat out over the railing. And he's not such a bad fellow, Morgen. You don't really know him.

Morgen's scuffs dropped from the soles of her feet and hung on her toes. I don't want to, she said. I couldn't ever get used to his looking at me as though he wished I didn't have any clothes on.

Fritz laughed and knocked the ashes out of his pipe. If that's a crime then I know a good many criminals, he said, and still laughing he turned toward the open door. You run on up to Mark's with your trowel.

I'll take it up this afternoon while you're having tea with Lubansky, she said after him. She tightened her hands on the railing and lifted herself and swung between the poles of her arms. She heard Fritz pulling out the easel and she let herself down and went to the door. He was behind the easel, looking at a handful of brushes. She looked at the brushes and at him and parted her hair low on the right side with the point of the trowel. The artist by himself? she said, laughing.

He shook his head and began slowly to separate the brushes. I think I'm going back to sign painting, he said. I thought of a fine idea all about how people could use trowels for combs. He smiled. Run along now and find something to do.

She laughed and didn't move. He hadn't touched a brush for so long, watching this preparation was like watching an experiment.

HIS eye caught the narrow blade of her shadow as it knifed the doorway and he cut the power on the lathe and said, Hello! in a loud voice. He saw her mouth make the shape of Hello, Mark, and he laughed and switched off the motor and said, I didn't hear you.

I said hello.

That's what I said too.

She held out the trowel. The ferrule's loose, Mark. I wonder if you could fix it.

He took the trowel without looking at it and put it on the bench. Sit down, he said, nodding to the stool. He leaned against the bench and looked at her, pushing his hands down into the bottoms of his pockets. She was wearing those old white sailor pants with dirty knees and a striped knit shirt and her hair was pushed back from her narrow face in long bright brush strokes and the sunlight hung in its loose ends. Her eyes wandered along the row of tools hanging over the bench and then they came back to his eyes and smiled and he nodded toward the stool again and said, Sit down.

No, thank you, she said, and her eyes wandered off again. What are you making?

He pulled himself up away from looking at her and

turned to the bench. He curved his hand around the cylinder in the lathe. Leg for a coffee table, he said. I'm just taking it down to the right size. Want to try it?

She shook her head and scooped up a handful of fine loose chips off the bench. She held the chips in her hand and felt their lightness and then she breathed at them and said, They haven't any fragrance, have they?

No, Mark said. This's maple. It's cedar you're so crazy about.

She opened her fingers and turned her hand over and the chips sifted down like heavy snow. Well, she said, looking up, thank you for fixing the trowel. There's no hurry about it.

I'll bring it down this evening, he said, following her to the door. How's the book coming?

Fine, thank you.

He leaned in the doorway and watched her go up the steps, her heels thin from the back and lifting off the soles of her scuffs at each step. When she reached the top and turned, he said, By the way, didn't you have a birthday yesterday?

Yes.

How does it feel to be twenty-one?

You ought to remember, she said. You're not that old.

So long, he said, laughing. He went back to the bench and switched on the motor and picked up the gouge. After a moment he began to sing very loud against the sound of his work.

MORGEN went around the house slowly and into the path that led down the hill to the wall, the sound of the lathe and of Mark's singing growing less and less distinct in her ears. She went along the wall to the place opposite the garden and lifted herself and lay at full length on the warm stones. Through the open windows of the house she could hear them talking, Fritz's slow deep voice, Lubansky's lighter voice and occasionally his laughter like a handful of coins shaken. Against the sky she saw Fritz's bright blue attentive eyes. Before yesterday she hadn't noticed that age had begun to blur the blue of his eyes a little. The blue was the same, but at the edge it had begun to seep into the white. Before yesterday she hadn't noticed that he moved now as though there were a brittleness within his body. The new year always exchanged gifts with the old. They had come into this year without her knowing what the year before had taken with it. The voices in the house lulled her and she felt herself drifting slowly toward a pause in consciousness and then without knowing she went into it wholly.

When she heard their voices again they were on the veranda and she waited and then they ceased as though a door had closed.

HE stood at the veranda railing until the sound of the motor died behind the shoulder of the hill. He thought, Thick yellow gloves on a fine warm day in August, and he went inside and picked up his pipe and put it between his teeth and stood looking out the window over the window seat. There was a still blue haze over the bay and in the air a scent of burning eucalyptus leaves. He clasped his hands behind his back and frowned against the weariness that had grown around him in the last hour. He wondered why talking tired him so much. He felt as though he were wearing on his head a tight cap of thin hot metal.

The back door opened and closed. Fritz? Morgen said. Shall I bring your milk?

Later, he said.

Did you have a nice time?

Very nice, he said. He's not a bad fellow.

She linked her arm in his and looked with him at the haze deepening to dusk in the air. She felt his weariness and said, Would you like me to read for a while?

He nodded and she went to get the manuscript and then they sat together on the window seat and she began to run through the pages.

We stopped on page ninety-six, he said.

She looked up and said, How do you always remember? and began quietly to read.

LATE in the afternoon Fritz tapped on her door and opened it. The light's getting bad, he said, I'm going to lie down now. You'd better stop too and go out for a walk.

All right, she said.

He was lying on his bed when she went past the open door, and she said softly, I won't stay out long, but he was already asleep. She went out and went swiftly down the steps and around the shoulder of the hill and then up past Mark's, past the little vacant house and on, breathing deeply and not letting herself slow her steps, until she was in the canyon. She rested then, looking down into the canyon, listening to the small sounds of birds moving unseen, a smaller sound of water and to the sound and movement of her breathing.

When she started back she left the trees and the soft young twilight of the canyon and went up a narrow trail onto the bare hill. She stopped again and stood watching the fog moving in the wind and then suddenly a voice close beside her said, It's marvelous, isn't it?

She turned quickly but the wind whipped her hair across her face. She pushed back her hair with both hands and saw a tall man standing beside her, smiling at her hands and her hair trying to escape them. He stepped up in front of her. There, he said. Now the wind's with your hair. You can put your hands back in your pockets.

She put her hands in her pockets and looked at him.

When he saw her eyes he stopped smiling and something in him seemed to hesitate, but he said, I'm lost. The fog's shut everything out. If I could find the campanile I'd be all right.

Why, there, Morgen said, nodding to it.

He glanced over his shoulder and laughed. As close as that! It looks like a little tent pitched in snow, doesn't it? I'd like to walk down the hill with you anyway.

Morgen looked at the campanile and then looked at him. All right. It isn't far.

He smiled and said, Thank you, as though he were clicking his heels. He wore a bright blue tie and when he turned it snapped out and lay shivering along the wind. He went beside her silently, looking out at the fog, looking often at her, looking at their feet walking in step. Finally he said, You know all the trails, don't you?

With my eyes closed.

That would mean you live close by.

About ten minutes from here, she said.

The trail narrowed and she walked ahead for a few moments and then it widened and he came up alongside her and said, If you live ten minutes from here we're in an awful hurry.

Well, Morgen said, when you walk this way it's twenty.

Let's walk this way then. He looked at her walking beside him with her hands in the deep pockets of her coat and her fair hair smoothed back away from her face by the wind. You know, he said, when I first saw you standing so still on the hill I thought you were a statue. What do you think about to keep as still as that? Wait, he said suddenly, and put out his hand and stopped her.

He looked at her so intently she smiled, but he said, Have you ever been modeled? I mean, have you ever had a portrait painted?

Oh, she said, many times.

Well, good Lord, he said, catching step with her. What do you know about that? Why, it's marvelous! I never heard of anything so marvelous! He walked looking at her. She was just the same, the long throat and the hair like fine white wine held to the light. Her face had the still listening look and her eyes were that clear deep blue over darkness. He pushed his hands down into the pockets of his jacket and stumbled over a stone. He wanted to stop her again and look at her eyes but he didn't. She was walking as though she were walking alone and he didn't dare change that.

AT the foot of the steps she stopped and said, I live here. If you'll follow this road down around the hill to the first street, you'll—

Later, he said, shifting his weight onto one foot. Right now I'm going to ask myself to tea. What do you say?

She looked at him. I'm sorry, we never drink tea and my father's resting.

I promise not to disturb your father.

She felt all along the insides of her pockets for a moment. All right, she said.

He followed her up the steps, looking at her thin ankles in calyxes of dark green wool socks worn over stockings, thinking what a marvelous thing it was. She went up the veranda steps quietly. At the door he said, My name's Royal St. Gabriel and yours is—

She said, Morgen Teutenberg, and opened the door.

He followed her inside, trying to make his footsteps sound as light as hers and she smiled at this and went to

Fritz's door and looked in and then closed the door softly. She slipped off her coat and said, Won't you sit down? and put her coat over the back of the divan and pulled down the cuffs of her sweater.

Royal said, Thanks, but didn't sit down.

Would you like beer or coffee?

He would have liked beer but he said, Coffee, because it would take longer to prepare.

She left him then and he stood perfectly still, looking out of his enchantment at the room. It was a long low room, ceiled in redwood, unfinished and beautifully seasoned and the rafters were decorated with red and blue and yellow sawtooth designs. He saw an easel standing under the skylight in a sort of alcove, lifted a couple of steps above the floor level. There was some very simple unfinished furniture. The divan was long and low and there was a narrow runner in front of it, woven in a sort of geometry lesson of many colors. The drapes at the windows were made of some heavy blue stuff and the divan was covered with it and the cushions were beginning to break along the edges. He went slowly to the fireplace and put his foot up on the hearth. He heard Morgen in the kitchen and he smiled at the fire, at his foot on the hearthstone. He couldn't believe it.

She came in carrying a tray and he started toward her, but she said, Will you move the table up to the hearth, please? and he turned back and moved the coffee table up. He pushed aside a tobacco jar and a pair of woolen socks and she put the tray down.

There, she said, sitting on the hearth. I'm not going to insist but I know you'd be more comfortable if you'd sit down.

He smiled and sat on the end of the divan nearest her. He ran his hands back over his short hair. I hate that jack-in-the-box business of jumping up every time a woman comes near me, he said. I always wait till the preliminaries're over. I'll have cream, thanks, no sugar. He took the cup and sat back, crossing his knees. She offered him a plate of little dark brown cakes and he took one and said, Thanks. A moment later he said, These are marvelous. Did you make them?

Oh, no.

He finished the cake and set his cup on the edge of the table and got his cigarettes out of his jacket pocket and drew two from the pack and gave one to her. I wish you had a piano, he said. I love to play for people I like and I think I like you. She was looking into her cup and she didn't look up and he leaned forward and poured himself more coffee and she poured in the cream. He lit their cigarettes. The room was filling up with shadows and he sat back and looked at her and said, Morgen, aren't you a little surprised we get along so nicely?

Her eyes came up out of their own shadow and she said, Why, no.

He smoothed his hand back over his hair. Well, some other time I'll ask if you're glad. He got his cup and drank some coffee and got another cake off the plate. Your father's the painter? She nodded and he finished the cake. These remind me of cakes I used to eat at tea-time when I was little.

She smiled and said, More coffee?

He shook his head, smiling, and rose. No, thanks. I'm going now.

She went with him to the door and looked out over his shoulder, feeling the air cold and moist on her face.

I'm awfully glad you let me come up, he said. He held out his hand. And I didn't thank you for rescuing me, did I? She looked at him and he looked down at her hand and smiled at it. Anyway, he said, I feel rescued. He hesitated over what he wanted to say and then decided to let everything stay exactly as it was. He unclasped his fingers and she put her hand into the pocket of her sweater. Good-bye, Morgen.

She took a step backward. Good-bye, she said.

WHEN he went in Barton was sitting in his chair at the window and Gildo was pouring whisky into a tall glass. He bowed to them. Gentlemen, he said.

Hello.

Have a drink? Gildo said.

He took off his jacket and lit a cigarette and said, No, thanks. He sat down at the piano and when his fingers touched the keys he felt a shock go through him to the soles of his feet. He sat frozen for a moment and then his body relaxed and he began to play.

Gildo said, Listen, Barton.

Royal lifted his hands abruptly and swung around. Say, Barton, he said, do you know anything about a fellow named Teutenberg, a painter?

Barton's eyebrows went up. The tall bearded Jesus of Berkeley?

That's the one, Royal said.

Barton rose and went over to the piano. Do I know anything about Teutenberg! He laughed.

Seriously I mean, Royal said.

Very seriously then, Barton said, looking at the ice in his glass, Fritz Teutenberg is probably one of the most important painters in the world today. As a man, nobody knows much about him but I gather he's rather a disagreeable old boy, very snooty. Lubansky gave half his fortune recently for one of his blonde young ladies. He has a penchant for blonde ladies, Teutenberg I mean, but no—

You're a dumb ox, Royal said, but thanks. He turned back to the keyboard and his hands settled. This, he said, glancing up at Barton, is for one of Teutenberg's blonde young ladies.

MORGEN closed the manuscript and put it on Fritz's knees.

Fritz rubbed his nose gently with the bowl of his pipe and said, Well, Morgen, you've done something as simple as those a b c's you never learned. They smiled at each other and she put her chin on her knees and waited and he ran his fingertips along the edge of the manuscript and felt a hard tight knot of pride working to untie itself in his heart. She had written of a child, she had worked with the intricate many-pieced pattern of childhood until it was a complete thing, separated from herself. She waited, listening to the wind around the eaves and in the acacias under the windows, and Fritz touched the manuscript again and said, Morgen, I've never been happier than I am at this moment. He put his pipe down and picked up the glass he had forgotten and drained it and then with his handkerchief he wiped the flecks of foam off his mustache, outward each way from the center. He lay back in his chair and stretched his legs out toward the fire. As I understand it, he said slowly, all a person has in this life to take with him to his Valhalla is the knowledge of happiness, his own and what he's managed in his lifetime to give others. He looked at the handkerchief, touched his mouth with it and then put it into his pocket. My torch, he said, is as bright right now as it will ever be.

A strong sweet warmth burned up from Morgen's heart, up through her veins, up into her throat, into her face. She took the thick manuscript off his knees and put her face there. Mine too, she said.

He smiled down at her and said a little tender thing not made of words but known to her.

WELL, he said, looking around the edge of the canvas.

Hello, Fritz.

You weren't gone long.

No, she said, smiling, I said good-bye to it before I left, in the privacy of my own room.

Fritz laughed and ruffled the hair at the back of his neck with his thumb. Well, it's off on its maiden voyage.

Its wanderjahr, Morgen said. She tossed her coat onto the windowledge and woke Isolde, who was sleeping there. Morgen bent down and smoothed her coat and Isolde stretched and began to unwind the spool of her purring. Did I wake you? Morgen said. Isolde looked at her and jumped to the floor and went on her soundless feet to the door. She lifted herself to full length on the door, leaning on her forepaws, and looked back at Morgen. Morgen opened the door for her and then went to the alcove steps and stood there. I still think you're doing a self-portrait, Fritz.

He shook his head and put down his palette.

Are you happy with it? she said.

Not particularly, he said. He couldn't understand why he tired so easily. It was disgusting. He wiped his hands on the tail of his smock, went down and across to the window seat, scowling against his weariness and the pain in his head. One thing you must never forget, he said. It's always harder to do a thing than to talk about doing it.

He had told her that a thousand times. She put her arm around his shoulders and kissed his forehead, finding with her lips the exact point of pain beating there. I know, she said.

Anyway, he said, lifting his shoulders and smiling up at her, we've got a book off to a publisher, even if we never finish the picture.

You know you'll finish it, she said.

He nodded and moved over, making room for her to

sit beside him. He looked for a long time at the back of the canvas. I wonder, he said slowly, how long it'll be before you hear from them.

Morgen laughed. Oh, it might be a month, she said. You're not going to be impatient about it, are you? He said nothing and she said, Patience was the first rule of life you tried to teach me, don't you remember?

He moved his hands. This is different, he said.

WELL, that's it, Fritz said, rubbing his cheekbone where the beard thinned. I've been postponing it for twenty years and now it's done.

Morgen nodded. She felt her heart lift and begin to beat upward into her throat. It was a large canvas, a deep green sea of shadows and on this sea a woman with child was lying on her side, with one arm stretched out above her head, the hand holding a small blue flower, the other arm bent to conceal her face.

This is what old Maurice used to call memory painting, Fritz said. I came in one afternoon and brought her the flowers and she wanted one to hold. It was hot that August and I drew down the window shades and after a while she slept, but she slept badly. Every few moments she woke and looked at me so strangely and asked if it were tomorrow. She was certain you were going to be born the next day and you were, very early, only you weren't the little Fritzl she'd planned for. It didn't end as we'd planned at all.

Morgen stood leaning against the wall, knowing her mother for the first time.

HE saw the postman leave the letterbox and he watched him until he was hidden by the shoulder of the hill and

then he rose and walked about impatiently. He went over
to his table behind the easel and looked at his clean
brushes and he picked up the palette knife and traced the
lines in the palm of his hand with the round of the blade.
He remembered very well her reading to him the first
scrap of poetry she ever wrote. He had it somewhere,
put away with a batch of old sketches. He thought about
getting them down off his wardrobe shelf but he drew out
the stool instead and sat down and tried to think why he
was so impatient. For one thing, he had decided there
might be a letter from that publisher in the box and then
he hadn't taken his rest as he'd promised to do when she
left, and being awake made the time long. Sitting there
he heard a light patter of rain on the skylight and he
looked up, but his eyes couldn't find raindrops on the
glass. He went out across the studio to the window seat
and looked out and he could see rain on the acacias and
he looked along the road and the road was darkening,
but while he looked the sound of rain ceased and he shook
his head and thought, If the leaves weren't wet and the
road dark like that I'd think I'd dozed and dreamed it.
He looked down at the letterbox again and knew very
surely this time that a letter was waiting there. He looked
down along the road once more and then he went to the
door and opened it and allowed his impatience to take
him too swiftly down the steps. His breath stopped and
then came in a rush and his sight blurred but he was at
the letterbox then and he opened it and saw several
letters. He reached into the box and his hand was shaking
and that angered him, but he drew out the letters and
looked through them with his sight unclear. He started
back up the steps.

Halfway up the steps his heart fluttered suddenly like
fingers on a drumhead and his breath left him and he
sagged against the air and almost fell. He thought, This is

dying, and he felt the hand close brutally over his heart and hold it. Then he found himself looking at the letters he still held in his hands and his vision was perfectly clear again. He smiled. He went on up the steps slowly, breathing with great care. It was no worse than it had been many times before.

Breathing carefully he went up onto the veranda and across it to the open door and inside. The room seemed airless and he put the letters on the window seat and went into his room and pushed open all the windows. The air felt fresh and alive on his face and he thought, Now I'll lie down for a little while, but on this thought's heels his breath sank again and the great hand enclosed his heart and he opened his mouth to breathe. Isolde, coming up onto the damp veranda on light fastidious feet, heard the sound he made and stared up at him. He hooked his fingers into the low neckband of his shirt and his hand hung there and somehow he turned and went the short way to the bed and sank onto it, knowing no thought.

HE saw her from the train step and excitement tightened his hand on the guard rail and lifted his weight up off his feet and lodged it in his heart. The gate slid open and he dropped off the still moving train and hurried after her, shouldering his way among other hurrying passengers. When he caught up with her he jerked off his hat and said her name.

She turned quickly. Why, hello.

He took her hand and held it tightly. So you actually came to meet me. How'd you guess?

Guess?

Never mind, he said. I'm fine, thanks. I'm not going to ask how you are. You're looking much too marvelous to be out alone like this. His heart got calmer and he took her arm as though his fingers were familiar with it. He looked at her and then looked away from her and saw everything all at once. I see you had some rain here this afternoon, he said.

Yes, only a little.

They crossed the street and he said, I've got to get some cigarettes, and a few doors down they went into a confectioner's shop and he went to the cashier's desk to get cigarettes and Morgen waited, watching two little girls who were watching her in the mirror and drinking earnestly through straws.

Royal came up behind her and bent his head down to hers and said, I'll tell you a secret. Right now I'm so happy I could sing. When you know me better you'll know that's as happy as I ever get.

Morgen smiled and he glanced at the two little girls on high stools and smiled at them in the mirror. He shook the money he held in his hand. Let's buy something, he said, looking around. Candy?

No, thank you, Morgen said. I never eat candy.

You never eat — I don't believe it. Everybody eats candy. You know, I've never bought candy for a girl and this's the day.

But Morgen went toward the door and he followed and reached around her to open it. Outside he lifted his shoulders and said, Can I sell you a cigarette? Nothing down, pay when you like.

Yes, thank you, Morgen said.

Are you always like this? Yes, thank you, no, thank you. Here. When she touched his hand to shield the match he held for her, excitement struck his heart again and he stood holding the match until its flame bit at his fingers. He dropped the match and struck another and Morgen, watching with clear unamused eyes, moved the keys in her pocket and said, We'll walk up through the campus. It's shorter that way. Were you really coming to see me?

He nodded and they walked on together. He looked at the hills standing like a great uneven wall at the end of the street. Are you glad, Morgen?

She nodded and said, We cross here.

You'd know the way with your eyes shut?

I think I would, she said.

You've lived here a long time, haven't you, Morgen? She didn't answer and in the middle of the street he stopped her and said quietly, I want you to understand something, Morgen. I like you so much I've forgotten if I ever really liked anyone else. I mean it. Are you glad about that, Morgen?

She took his arm quickly. Do you want to get run over?

No, he said, walking on, but I love being led. Anyway, you've forgotten we've just known each other a day, haven't you?

No, she said, I was thinking about it just now.

He took his hat from under his arm and straightened it and put it on his head and tried to think of another way to begin. He looked at her face in profile and wondered how he had let weeks go by, how he had almost stopped thinking about her at night when he turned out the light and every time he got tight and almost every time he touched a piano. To say something he said, Well, have you been busy these days?

Yes, she said.

How do you go about being busy? Do you paint too?

Oh, no, she said. I write.

That pleased him. Poetry?

She looked up, shaking her head. The hills look clean and lovely after the rain, don't they?

Do you go to school? She shook her head again and he said, Well, I know one thing, Miss Teutenberg. Whenever you did go to school you must have taken a very thorough course in the art of how not to make conversation. She smiled and walked smiling for a moment and he said, Morgen, how old are you?

Twenty-one.

They walked on, down over a little footbridge and up along a path and there was a cool wet smell of earth in the air and it made him feel fine and clean and younger than he was. This feeling went with him up the hill, walking between them like another person. Whenever he turned to look at Morgen he looked through that other person.

She stopped at the foot of the steps to look into the empty letterbox and halfway up she said, I've got a surprise for you.

You have? For me?

No, she said, smiling, for me, but you'll like it. She opened the door and said, Don't look around. Come over here and then turn around.

But he did look and his eyes caught and held on what he saw, and he couldn't move. Without moving his legs at all he felt himself going toward what he saw. He was cold along the length of his spine. He looked at Fritz's white hair splashed against the blanket and his beard very white on his blackened face and his body across the bed as though it had been dropped there. He heard Morgen coming and he bent down quickly. Morgen said, What're you doing? and he straightened with his stomach turning over and over and cold water running down his spine, but he got himself between Morgen and the doorway. He said, Morgen, and felt outward at his side for the edge of the door. Please don't go in, he said.

What's the matter? She didn't try to look around him but looked straight into his eyes.

He pulled the door shut and looked at her and knew what he had to say was already said. He saw her shudder once, all along the length of her body, and then she opened her mouth and he waited and finally the words came. Dr. Stauber, she said.

Royal shook his head. A doctor couldn't help, Morgen.

He put his arm around her shoulders. She pulled away from him and started toward the closed door but she stopped again and put her hands in her hair, close to her head behind and below her ears.

Morgen, he said, if you have any friends around here — He looked away from her white face and gnawed at his lower lip and then he saw Fritz on the bed and he said quickly, I'm going to take you over to the city with me, Morgen.

She was looking at the closed door, her hands clenched in her hair, her mind enclosed in a vacuum sound couldn't penetrate. She went with him out of the house. She heard him lock the door with her key without hearing.

THEY went into an elevator and after a moment they got out and walked along a corridor. Royal stopped her at a door. Here we are, he said. He tried the door and it was unlocked and they went in.

Gildo looked up and then rose.

Morgen, Royal said, looking at Gildo, this is my friend Mr. Gacetinni. Gildo, Miss Teutenberg.

Morgen looked at Gildo and Gildo bowed, holding his book down at the side of his leg, his forefinger marking his place.

Come over here, Royal said, taking her arm. She went with him and he turned his chair around so that sitting in it she would be closed away from the room. She sat down and Royal stood beside her, undecided. So much silence was suffocating him. He beckoned Gildo with his head and they went into the bedroom and Royal shut the door.

Listen, Gildo, he said, get some things packed. You're leaving for a couple of days.

Gildo smiled and sat on one of the beds. Certainly, he said.

Her father died this afternoon, Royal said.

Gildo's smile froze and slowly dissolved.

I couldn't leave her there alone with him, Royal said. We walked in and there he was, stiff as a poker. Hurry up. I've got to go back over to Berkeley. You might come back a little later and see how she is. No, don't do that either. She'll be all right. I don't know what else to do about her. Come on, hurry up, will you?

Certainly, Gildo said.

Royal went out and went to her and sat on the arm of the chair. He drew her head against his arm and held it there. I'm going now, Morgen, but I'll be back soon. You stay here. He bent and held his lips against her hair and then rose. Well, I'm going now. Call if you want anything. The phone's there by the door. I'll be back just as soon as possible. He stood there. He didn't know whether he should ask her permission to go ahead or not. He decided against asking. He didn't think she'd want anything to do with it. He knew he'd die if he didn't get away from her silence and the way she looked and breathed and sat there. He said, Good-bye, Morgen, and waited a moment more but her eyes did nothing. He walked slowly toward the door. He didn't know what she was made of, how she could sit there as quiet as sleep. What the hell was the name of that doctor? He stopped and tried to remember the name she had spoken but he couldn't think of it. Standing where he was he said, Morgen, what's your doctor's name? He waited, chewing at his lower lip, and then she said, Stauber. Nicholas Stauber.

Stauber, he said, and went on. In the pocket of his coat his nervous fingers found her silver key chain and he closed it on the three keys in his hand and went down the corridor to the elevator door and pressed the button. Oh Jesus, he thought. He sighed and hunched his shoulders under the weight of his topcoat.

HE closed the door behind him and put the traveling-case down and said, Morgen? and she lifted her head. She was sitting just as he had left her. Her face looked thinner in the pale reflected light from the window. Great wings of shadow covered her eyes. He went down awkwardly on his knees before her and took her hands, his warm and moist from gloves, hers cold and unalive as stone hands. He knelt there for a long time. I brought some things over for you, he said quietly. What I could find easily. I called your doctor. Everything's taken care of. But we'll talk about that later. He pressed her hands and rose, standing before her on his cramped legs. She lifted her head and he felt her eyes lift to his and suddenly he knew what to do. Without lighting the room he went to the piano and began very softly to play.

HER hands lay on the blanket he had drawn over her and her eyes moved in the dark without seeing. She went back and forth across the limited space of the moment, not daring to take the step backward nor the one forward. Time stopped because she ceased to be aware of time. She was still deaf and dumb and sightless in the dark vacuum of shock.

AND in the room beyond Royal lay on the too short sofa and smoked another cigarette and finished another whiskey and soda. He wondered again if she had fallen

asleep and he shifted his tired back and wondered suddenly about the power that maneuvered fates. Was there a
power like that? His tongue, moving against the edges of
his teeth, felt blistered from too much smoking and he
put out the cigarette and stretched. At the windows he
could see the sky pale and without color, and without
looking at his watch he knew it was morning. He stretched
his arms and back again, and then, folding his arms across
his chest, fell suddenly into heavy sleep.

HE signed the check and tipped the waiter out of his pocket
and the waiter went out and he stood by the table and waited.
He had heard her moving about behind the door and now
he watched the doorknob and when he saw it turn he jumped
as though he'd been caught with his eye at the keyhole. He
jerked his hands out of his pockets and bent over the table.

She saw him pouring coffee and she went to him and
he handed her a cup. He filled the other cup without looking up. There's toast and jam, he said, and liver and bacon.
Won't you have some?

No, thank you, she said, but I'd like a cigarette.

He put his cup down and got her a cigarette and lit it
for her and saw her eyes go slowly like sleepwalkers from
the flame of the match to his fingers, along his hand to
the wrist, thick and darkened on the back with hair,
along it to the blue band of his cuff. He dropped the
match into the ashtray on the table and saw her eyes lift
for an instant and really touch his eyes, and his heart
lifted, though she turned away and went toward the
window, carrying her coffee and trailing loose blue veils
of smoke behind her. She stood beside the chair at the
window, smoking but not drinking her coffee, looking
curiously at the boundaries of this new world.

Royal watched her for a few moments and then he

sat down at the little table and uncovered the dishes and served himself and began to eat.

She heard the silver-on-china sound of his eating and watched the traffic moving in the street below.

Morgen, he said, I wish you'd eat a bite.

She turned and came back and he rose quickly and drew out the other chair for her. Sitting opposite him she looked at the coffeepot and at the liver and bacon and at the little pot of jam. I don't believe it, she said slowly, but it's true or I wouldn't be here, would I? She spoke slowly as though she were speaking a strange new language. She took hold of the edge of the table and her eyes searched his face and went back to the table again. I can't believe it could happen so suddenly, but I've known for a long time it could happen any time. Dr. Stauber told me it could happen any time. I've seen it begin to happen, all the blood in his face suddenly and that terrible lost look in his eyes and his breath held back.

Royal thought she was going to stop breathing. She seemed to sink down into some hollow within herself where breath wasn't needed and he saw himself grow distant and indistinct in her eyes.

Then she breathed again. She took her hands off the table and locked them together tightly and her eyes grew very bright in her narrow face. If I had been there, she said, if I had known and stayed with him.

No, Royal said, I'm sure it's better you weren't there.

It's just as if I'd dreamed it, isn't it? Coming into this room this morning and seeing you pouring my coffee —

Royal looked at her and started to speak but no words were there. He knew words didn't matter, whether he answered her or not didn't matter.

SHE looked down once and then turned, walking away from the grave with fast undirected steps. She wanted to run somewhere but there was no strength in her legs and she hesitated and pressed her hands over her face, not knowing where to go.

Royal caught up with her and took her arm and turned her back toward the driveway. This way, he said.

Why did I come? she said into her hands. Oh, why did I come?

We'll be gone in two minutes, Royal said.

She walked with her hands covering her face, but she saw the grave dug in the darkness against her eyes.

Here, Royal said. He opened the door of the car and guided her inside and hurried around and got in beside her.

She sat with her shoulders bent, her hands pressed over her face. She felt the car move and she knew when they were out of the cemetery. The pressure of her hands lessened. The pavement was smooth under the tires, the tires sang, the sound of the motor and of the tires on the pavement acted like an opiate. She became suspended in a dark half-sleep.

When she woke the car was motionless on a cliff above an empty beach. She looked out to sea and then at Royal and then beyond him again out to sea. She felt separated from herself, she felt herself on the horizon and at the same time she was sitting beside Royal.

Want to go down on the beach? he said.

She nodded and they got out of the car and she went ahead of him down the yellow cliff. On the beach they stood looking out to sea, their eyes narrowed against the wind and light. When she walked away from him he looked after her for a moment, her hair blowing in the wind, her

30

skirt molded to her thigh, her narrow feet sinking into the sand.

He sat down and scooped up a handful of sand and watched it sift through his fingers. It had happened to him. He was detached from it now because of what had happened and he could think about it and wonder over it. Somehow it had been saved for him to know. He scooped up another handful of sand. He had only to stay close to her until time wore away the sharp point of grief and then she would know with him.

He didn't see her come but she was beside him suddenly. He looked up and smiled and put his hand over her instep and held it closely. Shall we go?

Yes, she said. I'm glad we came here, Royal.

He got to his feet and followed her up the cliff.

SHE sat low on the seat listening to the monotonous sound of the motor. Darkness softened by fog had drawn down around them. The headlights cut two blunt wedges out of the night but the darkness beyond was unknown and larger than it really was because it was unseen. She held her cold hands together and let her eyes close. The sound of the motor, so long in her ears, had become a part of her.

And behind them, somewhere on that hillside, fog was fingering the wilted flowers and it was still, except for the wind and an echo of weeping.

SHE went up the steps while he paid off the taxi. She had been away only three days but the terrace looked unkept and the steps and the veranda were strewn with leaves. It was like coming to a long-vacant house. She waited at the door for Royal. He came up the steps with her traveling-case and some packages. She unlocked the door and thought, It will break now, the thin ice, the dream thinness.

It was an empty house. She walked into it slowly with hollow footsteps, feeling its emptiness, not looking at anything. Royal followed, setting the traveling-case on the window seat, tossing his hat down beside it. He took off his topcoat and went quietly into the kitchen with the packages. In the kitchen he took off his jacket and turned up his shirt cuffs. He washed his hands in cold water and began to look for a frying pan.

THEY sat on the divan with the coffee table at their knees and ate little smoked oysters and scrambled eggs and thin toast. The fire made a great warmth and brightness and they lived in that, closed in its light away from the house. Once Royal said lightly, It's at it again, and Morgen looked up toward the small murmur of sound on the skylight. They drank chablis, which Morgen didn't like, and coffee afterward and sat watching the rain running thinly down the windows. They smoked and watched the fire and looked at the rain on the windows and all the time Royal knew she was listening, all her nerves were stretched across the sound of rain toward a sound in the house. He said nothing. He knew when she ceased to listen. Without looking at her he felt the tired quivering surrender of the nerves, the beginning of rest. He took a deep breath and said, I don't like to go but I've got to, Morgen. He sat up and took her hands and looking at them said, I hate to go but I know you'll be all right. He turned her hands over and said, Morgen, I don't know how you're — I mean, if you need money now.

She smiled thinly at him and took one of her hands away and, leaning across the table, put the cork in the bottle of wine and hit it lightly with her palm flattened. No, thank you, she said. I have enough money.

I just wanted to be sure. My mother left me some money that I haven't had to touch. If you ever need it, Morgen, it's yours. He rose and drew her up and they went to the window seat and he put on his muffler and his coat and picked up his hat. He took her hand again. May I come over tomorrow?

Yes, she said. She walked with him to the door. Standing at the door she looked up at him with the first tenderness in her eyes. She drew his hand up and held it against her face and said, Dear Royal.

A dark sweet wine flowed through his veins. His heart stopped and then plunged and then he found himself standing in the rain on the veranda.

Morgen closed the door and stood leaning against it, listening, looking at all the shadowed places in the room. She thought, It will break now, and walked slowly away from the door toward the fireplace. She sat on the edge of the hearth with her back to the fire and wondered how it could be that she was there unchanged, alone with the sound of rain, the room unchanged around her, everything just the same but not the same because he wasn't there.

LITTLE pools of water dripped from his raincoat and began to mark the floor all around him. He ran one of his wet hands across his wet face and snapped the water off his fingers. My God, he said, I didn't know a thing about it till I opened the paper last night. Why didn't you tell me?

I don't know.

I couldn't believe it. I didn't know what'd happened to you. I called Stauber and he said you were in the city and I had to think everything was all right but I didn't know what the hell to do. He set his tightened fist into the palm of his hand as carefully as though he were pressing a seal. I know talking doesn't help, Morgen.

No, she said.

When I saw the light I came right down.

I knew you would, Mark.

He looked at her. I've been keeping Isolde. She was nervous. She still is a little.

I'll come up and get her in the morning, Morgen said.

Well, I won't stay. Let me know when I can do anything. He pushed both hands down into his pockets and went backward toward the door. I know words don't mean a damned thing, Morgen. He fastened the top button of his raincoat and opened the door and said, If you need help burning any midnight oil, let me know.

SHE woke from a long nightmare of insecure and broken sleep and lit a cigarette and lay thinking that now her days were dripping trees and darkness, thinking that some day she would learn not to wake suddenly in the night wanting to call his name, not to want to go to his door and stand listening. She would learn those things. Other people had learned them.

The rain had stopped but outside her windows the heavy drops fell from the branches and the darkness was alive with this low endless weeping. She put out her cigarette and turned on her side to face the window and after a while she slept again, but not with rest, and at six o'clock she got out of bed. She bathed and made her coffee and dressed, all in one continuous process of haste. This left no time to be held and shaken restlessly in her hands like pennies.

She left the door unlocked in case Royal should come before she returned. She walked swiftly but without destination. The streets were wet under the trees and the trees were damp and dark, their branches shining darkly. Few people were out so early but she looked intently at each person she passed, wishing in despair that it were possible to put herself into someone else so swiftly the transmutation would be complete before anyone was aware. She wished she could stand quite still and watch herself walk off down the street in another body.

She walked until she grew hot and tired and then she turned back. She came down around the hill, past the little vacant house, past Mark's and stopped at the gate and said softly, Isolde, and Isolde showed herself instantly on Mark's balcony, looking down at Morgen and making little soft cries. She leapt onto the roof below the balcony and onto the fence and disappeared under the shrubs that lined the fence but the little soft excited cries came nearer and then she was under the gate, turning and turning about Morgen's ankles.

Morgen bent and lifted her. Did you think I'd never come for you? Were you lonely? Poor Isolde.

They went on down the hill, the long way around, talking softly to each other all the time. They were half-way up the steps when Morgen looked up and saw Royal standing on the veranda.

Good morning, he said, smiling down at them.

Hello, Royal. She went up onto the veranda with Isolde, not smiling but glad he was there. You came early, she said.

He held himself there against the railing. Yes, I've got to go right back. I've got a luncheon date I forgot all about and it's too important to chuck. He smiled down at Isolde. I found the latchstring out so I went in and made myself at home. He reached out and brushed Isolde's ruff with the tips of his fingers. Isolde of the golden hair, he said tenderly, and then in the same voice he said, I've thought of you a thousand times since yesterday, Morgen.

She looked at him gravely and said, Did you? and turned toward the open door. She stopped in the doorway and stood still.

He had built a fire and on the table against the wall he had arranged a great cluster of deep gentle blue asters in an unpolished copper bowl.

WELL I've got to dash, Morgen.

You shouldn't have bothered coming over, she said, for such a little while.

He smiled. That was sweetly said. Oh, there's your postman. Wait half a minute and I'll run down and get your mail for you.

I'll go down with you, she said.

They went together down the steps to the letterbox and he stood playing with the cord on his hat while she got out the letters and looked at them. There were four. Her hands and her eyes paused over the second one and a small pebble of excitement dropped into her heart. She slipped her forefinger under the flap of the envelope and tore it open and took out the letter. This is from Mr. Newhall, she said. Royal looked at her and saw her grave face soften in surprise. Wire? she said reading. I didn't get his wire. She finished the page and looked up at Royal. A shaft of light had struck her eyes and splintered their darkness. He likes it very much, she said.

I'm sure he does, Royal said, smiling, but what?

He's going to publish it, she said. My book.

Well, good Lord! Royal said. Here, let me look at you. Her eyes lifted, looked at him and went back to the letter.

He knew then that he had no real place in this

moment. It's wonderful, Morgen, and I'm terribly thrilled and proud of you but I've got to dash or I'll miss my train. I'll be over tomorrow, some time in the afternoon. All right?

She nodded and at that moment Mark came around the hill, walking in the middle of the road with his hands in his pockets and his mouth shaping a whistle but no sound there. He saw them. Well, he said, hello, there.

Oh, hello, Mark. She glanced from Mark to Royal and said, Mark Strauss, Royal St. Gabriel.

Royal and Mark looked carefully at each other, nodded, looked at each other again. I just missed Isolde, Mark said. She come home?

Yes, Morgen said, I got her early this morning.

Okay, Mark said. He nodded to Royal again and started back down the road but suddenly Morgen said after him, Mark, Newhall's going to publish my book.

He swung around and looked at her. I think it's going to rain, he said, and then laughed. My God, Morgen, you might give a thing like that a break! He came back and put his hands on her shoulders and looked at her for a moment. It's already done a swell thing to you, he said. Congratulations.

Royal rolled his hat brim into a neat brown cigar and smiled and Morgen smiled up at Mark and he said, It's swell, and put his hands in his pockets again and started back down the road and this time he continued and they watched him, and Royal, looking at his wide back, said, Husky young devil. Who is he?

He lives in that house up there, she said. He's our framer.

Royal jammed his hat on his head. Lord, he said, I've got to run. It's wonderful about your book. He started off down the road, walking sidewise and unevenly, smiling back at her. Good-bye, Morgen. You'll have to tell me all about it tomorrow.

Thank you for the lovely flowers, Royal.

He made a gesture with his right hand that ended at the crown of his hat. Good-bye, he said, lifting the hat.

WHEN she went in she went to Fritz's door and stood with Mr. Newhall's letter open in her hand. Fritz, she thought, are you happy now because of this? Do you know? She opened the door and went in. She hadn't been in the room for four days. She crossed the room to the bed, neat under its gray blanket. She sat there holding the letter, slow tears gathering in her eyes. She knew now what it was. He had taught her the language of silence but they had never been without another way of speech and now there was no way out of herself to him.

She rose and went to the window, carrying the letter. She pushed open the window over the veranda and, leaning against the frame, cried with no will ever to cease crying.

SHE pulled the divan close to the hearth and sat with the pad of letter paper on her knees and wrote a note to Mr. Newhall. When she finished that she opened the other letters that had come in the morning and lain unopened all day. One was a letter from Lubansky, a letter of condolence. She put the letter into its envelope again and tossed it into the fire. She looked at the return addresses on the other two letters and tossed them into the fire after Lubansky's.

There was a fresh pot of coffee sitting on the hearth and she poured herself a cup and sipped it slowly, looking into the fire. How did anyone dare to write a letter like that? People she scarcely knew. Writing a letter like that was like speaking to a stranger in the street. She put the empty cup on the hearth beside the coffeepot and tried to think how she was going to begin living over an end of life. And out of this thought's silence an evening came back to her out of the summer just ended. Dr. Stauber was with them at dinner and afterward they sat long at table, talking a little, resting comfortably in silence. The candles were black and their wax had spilled over and hardened along their sides so that they stood in their sockets like motionless black dancers. Fritz got up to get a fresh pipe and when he came back Dr. Stauber picked up the warm pipe he had just finished and said, Fritz, it's about time you stopped stoking these things twenty-four hours a day. She smiled at Fritz and went back to studying the black dancers and she didn't know if Fritz filled the fresh pipe or not, it meant nothing then, but later, when they left the table and while Fritz was in the bathroom, Dr. Stauber sat down slowly beside her on the hearth, sighing with the effort of lowering his heavy fat body and said, Morgen, you're a sensible girl. I want you to see to it that he cuts down his smoking. If you don't I'll have to do something about it and that wouldn't be nearly so pleasant. He doesn't seem to realize that every breath he draws comes through the bowl of a pipe. He's an old man. She laughed at that. Fritz old? Dr. Stauber looked at her and then Fritz came back into the room and that was all. She saw him coming in, pausing at the table to take a grape from the bowl between the two black candles, coming toward them, grinding at the grape seeds with his strong teeth.

Now for a moment the deep inward weeping overcame her and her hands made the blind wandering search toward her face but she checked them, pressed them together on her knees and plunged her naked eyes into the bright heat of the fire and held them there until they dimmed and escaped in pain under their lids.

She woke an hour later, unaware at first that she had slept. The fire had burned to a deep pink mound of coals. She stretched and thought of putting more wood on the fire, but she rose instead and went to the windows. She stood looking out into the dark. The sky had cleared, uncovering the small white stars.

HE pulled the ashtray nearer and began to draw horizontal lines in the ashes with a paper match. That morning, he said, I lost my belief in God and man, especially Royal St. Gabriel. Lord, did I get panned. They didn't know whether I played worse than I wrote or wrote worse than I played. It's still a toss-up. Anyway, it was a beginning and it convinced Dad I wasn't just having a good time for myself. Eventually some of the critics did say nice things about that concerto and I got my first spot on the radio and everything was marvelous. He drew more slowly and carefully with the match. Then one day I went to see a fellow and I saw a picture in his office. It was a picture of a girl and I think I fell in love with her then and there, Morgen, but my life went along and then I walked into the most wonderful day of all. I saw that girl standing on a hill. Well, that made everything exactly right. He didn't look up. He drew lightly with the match and Morgen watched him and waited and after a while the waitress came over and said, Would you like more coffee? And Royal said, Yes, another pot please, and then he looked at Morgen. Well, he said, that's the story of my life, more or less. You know all I could remember to tell you about myself. He dropped the match into the ashtray and pushed it back and laced his strong hands together and looked at her. I don't even know if you enjoyed your luncheon.

Oh, yes, Morgen said, very much.

I don't even know the title of your book.

It's *The Island.*

The Island, he said softly. His thin face glowed as though a sun had touched it. Morgen, did you have an island too?

She shook her head. Not like yours, Royal. Mine was only a little white rug.

For an instant the same sun that touched his face touched hers. They smiled.

Then the waitress came with the coffee and the clock in the campanile a block away chimed two o'clock, the two big bell-like notes droning out and vibrating into the still afternoon air.

HE stood in the doorway, holding his left wrist with his right hand. I'm so glad I came this morning, he said. I've never had a real Monday.

But I've finished, she said. She was wearing a blue knitted headband that held her hair back from her face and ears.

No, he said, something tells me they have to hang in the sun and dry.

She looked up smiling. Do you want to hang them up?

With all my heart, he said. I never wanted to do anything so much.

She laughed and he had never heard her laugh, all the music of her voice gathered into her throat and tossed upward. He unbuttoned his jacket and took it off. They ought to put that up in bottles, he said slowly, and sell it in every drugstore.

Put what in bottles?

Your laughter.

Come on, she said. You have to clean the line first. Here's the cloth.

She opened a cupboard door under the sink and took out a small basket with a looped strap fastened to its handles and a small wire hoop fastened to the strap. The basket held clothespins. Royal looked everything over and picked up the basket and followed her out of the kitchen and down the steps onto a flagged terrace.

All right, she said, smiling. She sat down on the steps and drew her knees up and held her ankles in her hands.

He cleaned the line carefully and then went back to the basket and picked up a wad of damp white cloth, shook it out and held in his hands a pair of small white panties. He smiled at them and bent with a red face to get a pin from the basket, dropped the pin and stooped again.

Hook the strap over the line, Morgen said from the steps, and then slide the basket along as you go.

That's an idea.

Mark thought of it, she said. He put the hook on.

Royal put the hook over the line and, pushing the basket of pins ahead of him, pinned up four pairs of white panties, two little blue and white striped jerseys, eight handkerchiefs and a blue smock.

That's upside down, Morgen said. It dries better if the sleeves are down.

He said, Corrected, and repinned the smock and then surveyed his work. Everything looks too little for you, he said, smiling. He rubbed his palms together and walked slowly across the flags to the steps and stood before her. She was smiling, but he didn't smile. He stood with his weight on one foot, his head dropped forward a little. His eyes became a deeper darker brown and he said simply, Morgen, I love you so much.

She looked at him for a long time, saying the words over to herself with his voice, but gradually from within she felt a tightening, a closeness in herself away from him and she couldn't think of anything to say out of that closeness in herself that wouldn't hurt him. She didn't want to hurt him but she wanted him to know what it was she felt. She held up her hand and made room for him to sit on the step beside her. Royal, she said.

It doesn't call for any sort of an answer, he said. I just wanted to say it, I had to. You don't have to answer. He looked at the things out on the line moving slightly in the wind and he smiled a little, very happily and from within, and folded her hand inside both his hands. Such beautiful clean hands. He smiled. You know, you're going back to the city with me when I go. Did you know that? I'm going to take you to dinner and watch you eat a steak as big as one of those flagstones. I don't think you're eating at all these days. It shows all over you, even in these well-washed hands.

She looked at his hands holding her hand. Not today, Royal, but some other day I will.

Today, he said.

It's sweet of you to want to stuff me full of steak, she said, smiling, but not today.

He smiled and looked at the things moving on the line and at their hands held together. He was contented in himself now and not impatient. He looked at the terrace and up over the wall at Mark's house and at the little house beyond with blank windows and wisteria falling matted from its roof like uncombed hair. He nodded toward it. That little birdhouse vacant?

Yes, Morgen said, it's been vacant for months.

Suppose I take it.

She looked at him to see if he were speaking seriously. He wasn't. You wouldn't like it, she said. Your piano would completely fill any room in it.

Too bad. Imagine being able to whistle you out to the wall every morning.

A man and a woman killed each other in it once, Morgen said. He killed her and then himself I think. That was years ago.

Well! So their ghosts scare tenants away for ever after?

Oh, no. This time it's been vacant longer than it ever was.

Well I might decide to take it, after all, he said. Sure you won't have dinner with me?

Not this time, Royal, but thank you.

He rose and stood looking down at her. Well, Mahomet did it, he said. Next time I come over I'll bring the steak to you.

ALL I know's what's on the tag, lady.

Morgen stood holding the edge of the door, looking from his face to the radio. But it's a mistake, she said. I didn't order a radio. I don't know anything about it.

Oh, he said, swinging the little radio over to his left hand. It slipped my mind for a minute. He reached into one of his jacket pockets and drew out an envelope. Here, he said, maybe this'll help.

She took the envelope and opened it. She saw Royal's name at the foot of the page and, without reading the body of the letter, moved aside and said, All right, bring it in.

The boy entered, looking around with his quick practiced eyes. Any particular place you want it? That bookcase be all right? He nodded to the low center section of the shelves along the wall opposite the fireplace.

That'll be all right, Morgen said.

Got an outlet handy?

Yes, at the left end.

He set the radio on the shelf and reached into his jacket pocket and at the same time bent to locate the outlet. That's fine, he said. I'll take the antenny right up this panel and around. He indicated its circuit with his shoulder. He worked fast, brushing frequently at an oily lock of hair that fell over his forehead. I'll slip the cord down behind the shelves, he said. That way you won't ever have it under your feet.

Morgen sat watching him. It would be lovely to hear Royal playing here in the room, invisible to her. She had never thought seriously about a radio. Mark had one, Dr. Stauber had one, but she had never thought seriously of having one herself.

In a very short time it was installed and a little light winked on and gleamed like an eye, and the boy, smiling at her across his shoulder, brought a loud wailing voice into the room, banished it immediately, brought chamber music very clear and intimate as breathing and discarded it. Well, he said, there she is. Take your pick. He began gathering up his tools.

Would you mind, Morgen said, going toward the radio, showing me just how to play it?

The boy looked at her blankly and brushed at his lock of hair. Why, sure, he said.

SHE had memorized the station call letters from the card the boy had left with her and at five minutes of five, anticipating difficulty, she went to the radio and dialed Royal's station. A woman's voice came softly into the room and Morgen went back to the table and reread Royal's letter to make sure she had the right station. It was the right station so she lit a cigarette and sat on the divan to wait. She waited what seemed to her a long time.

It seemed so strange to have this woman's voice in the room with her. She had got used to feeling another presence without voice and now there was a voice but the presence was not there. She didn't think she particularly liked having a radio. It was disturbing, like someone talking to her from another room. A chime sounded and she got up to get an ashtray. A man's voice was speaking now and suddenly she heard Royal's name. The man's voice said, Mr. St. Gabriel will play first, from manuscript, one of his own compositions entitled Morgen.

Morgen felt as though all at once a thousand tiny needles had picked at her face. Her eyes fastened themselves to the radio and then the first note came softly as a leaf falling and she was in his hands.

AND Royal, at the piano but not really there, felt it and felt tears come to his eyes and he smiled like a man smiling in sleep.

FIRST I'll put the steak in the icebox, he said.

Royal, did you really bring steak?

He lifted the big package. Do you doubt it? He laughed at it and at her and went out into the kitchen, and when he came back he sat in the opposite end of the divan and said, Now.

She unclasped her hands and stretched one of them out along the back of the divan and looked intently at it for a moment and then looked at him sitting with his arms folded, his eyes warm and bright in the firelight. You did a strange thing this afternoon, she said slowly. When you played the Morgen I saw myself, I knew myself. I felt as though I were in your hands and that you were showing me myself.

He held his arms across his chest and breathed carefully against them. I'm glad, Morgen.

She lifted her hand off the back of the divan and looked at it again. It was so lovely of you to think of sending me the radio, Royal.

He shook his head and laughed. Lovely like a fox. But anyway it'll be company for you. He felt his breathing grow calmer against his arms. Now let's talk about you. What's been happening to you? What've you been doing since I saw you?

I haven't done anything, she said. The book contracts came and last night Dr. Stauber came in for a little while and this morning Mark and I walked up to the Big C. That's all.

Royal nodded, wondering about that fellow Mark, wanting to ask about him but not asking. On this wondering a quiet came down over them. Morgen thought, If he were what he was in the music, if it weren't necessary to wind yourself up for him like a doll and talk, and Royal watched the firelight rubbing soft warm tips of fingers along her throat and over her face and wished he knew everything there was to know about her, what she talked about when she was with Mark, what her life had been, every moment of it, what would happen now if he began to make love to her, what she would say, what would happen to her eyes. He knew more than anything else he dreaded seeing that cool closed look come into her eyes but he knew too that the longest part of waiting was over now because he had told her he loved her and she had listened and not really closed away.

When the campanile chimed seven o'clock they looked at each other and he put out his wrist and said, Already? He rose and stood with his ear turned toward the kitchen door. Morgen, would you listen to that fellow out there in the icebox? Come on, let's go let him out.

She rose smiling and went with him into the kitchen.

SHE sat with her hair pushed back behind her ears and her cigarette making a long curved ash over her fingers. An hour before she had come out of thin disturbed sleep feeling mutilated and she had lain with closed eyes, dreading the light as though it would show a part of her gone. That feeling persisted, though she was there untouched, no part of her gone, the day growing up around her idleness. She picked herself up from within the small part of her back and, lifting her hands to the typewriter, wrote rapidly, Today he has been a month in the ground.

She stared at the words and then beyond them and she saw that awful moment again, his going down into the ground. But now it was a moment outside her and she could look at it. She reached for her cigarette and rolled it carefully away from its ash but left it burning in the tray. She put her elbows on the edge of the table and propped her face in her hands and thought, If I could write out of myself everything I know of him he would be here gathered all into me, he would be born again and held in my hands.

She knew, lighting a fresh cigarette, what she was going to do. In the chest of drawers and on the wardrobe shelf in his room there were bundles of old letters, old sketches with notations, a few old photographs. She pulled the sheet of paper out of the typewriter and went out into his room.

It was a small room holding much light, a tall unpainted chest of drawers, a thong bottomed chair, a narrow bed covered with a gray blanket and the wardrobe, which was built into the room itself. He had never allowed her to clean his room nor in any way to alter its simplicity. He had asked her never to bring flowers into it. It's better to see flowers growing, he said, just as it's better to see birds in the air above the reach of hands.

She looked tenderly at everything in the room. She had learned to see again, but very slowly as a wound heals. She could lie on his bed now, her hands locked under her head, her eyes following a shaft of sunlight across the wall. She could put work away from her and lie idle without fear.

HE stood squarely in front of her. You're not even hospitable. First we have to damage our knuckles before we get in, then you make us wait ten minutes while you go change those dirty pants I would be ashamed to be seen in. Morgen glanced away from him to Royal but Royal was smiling. I want to tell you something important, Gildo said in the same light voice. He swung a chair around and sat down directly in front of her, leaning forward and resting his elbows on his knees, careful of the creases in his trousers, lacing his pale thin hands together. Does it ever occur to you that if Royal were to open a can of sardines there would somehow be fish for a multitude? Well, that's the sort of man he is. She looked at him more closely, not amused, and he unclasped his hands and began to rub the ball of one thumb over the knuckle of the other. He was perfectly still except for his thumb. I want to tell you something else, he said. It's exceedingly foolish of you to treat a man so badly who loves you so much.

She looked at Royal and this time he wasn't smiling, he was getting slowly to his feet. He came slowly toward them. What is this? he said.

Gildo smiled at Morgen. I'm telling her what a beautiful person you are under your homely skin.

Thanks very much, Royal said, but skip it, if you don't mind.

Surely you understand, Gildo said softly, watching Morgen, that it was all a joke.

She looked at him with nothing at all in her face and then she rose. I'm sorry I can't go driving with you, Royal.

Why, Gildo said, I was only talking to amuse you.

Come on, Royal said. Get your hat. We didn't come to spend the weekend. Gildo lifted his shoulders very slightly and left them to get his hat off the window seat and Royal said quietly, I'm sorry about it. I'll come over tomorrow and we'll have a walk and dinner some place. All right?

She hesitated. All right. About five.

Fine, he said.

Gildo was watching them and when they turned he smiled and said, If you could see how beautiful you two are together.

Royal got his hat. As a matter of cold fact, he said, Gildo got a new car yesterday. He just wanted to show it off. But she ignored Gildo and reference to him as completely as though he hadn't ever come into the room. Royal said quickly, Tomorrow, and put his hand between Gildo's shoulder blades and went toward the door.

She closed the door on them and went back into Fritz's room and sat on the floor among the sketches and letters she had taken from the chest of drawers, but something wasn't there that had been closed in the room with her before they came. She sat there for a while, turning over papers, looking at sketches, taking the letters out of their frayed envelopes.

Finally she gave it up and went outside and found Isolde sleeping on the wall and too lazy with sleep to be disturbed. Morgen sat beside her on the wall for a while and then she lifted her feet and pivoted and jumped down on the other side and went up the path to Mark's.

She heard him singing and went around the house to

the shop door and went down the steps. He was standing at the gluepot and he smiled when he saw her but went on stirring the glue. Come in, he said. He looked at her hands empty at her sides. Didn't you bring it?

She looked at her hands. Bring what?

That mousetrap, he said, stirring the glue. I thought maybe it needed a little hinge fixed or something.

She went nearer, looking from her hands to the glue-pot, up to his placid face.

Haven't you got a mousetrap down there? he said, lifting the paddle and looking at the brown ribbon of glue. No? He wiped the paddle handle with a rag. I been seeing so many visiting young men on your doorstep lately I thought — Hey, where you going?

She was gone.

WHAT I mean is, Royal said, trying to keep his voice down, when you saw she didn't like it you should've shut up. Why the hell I took you —

Gildo turned a corner. He threw away his cigarette with a vicious little jab of his gloved hand at the air. All the same, he said calmly, you will never get anywhere with that girl.

Who the hell wants to get anywhere? What business of yours is it anyway?

Gildo laughed. Don't act like a child. No, she's very beautiful — like a bottle of champagne perfectly iced but no champagne in the bottle.

You can let me out right here, Royal said, taking hold of the door.

I hate to see you act so foolish, Gildo said. What's got into you? Roy, let's stop and get a drink.

Royal jerked at the brim of his hat and stared straight along the long nose of the car. You can't get a drink up here, he said. There's an ordinance or something.

Gildo turned another corner. You see? he said smiling, no wine in the bottle.

Royal half turned on the seat and his right arm twitched. I told you once, God damn you! He moistened his lips that had got as dry as sand. You pack your junk as soon as you get back, or I'll pack mine, I don't give a damn which. He reached down and took hold of the brake lever. Now let me out at the next corner.

AFTER his second cocktail he was so full of all the things he wanted to say to her he had to say them, though he had made himself believe he wouldn't say them until he knew she wanted to hear them, but now he had to say them. He took hold of the stem of his glass and leaned forward over the table and said, Morgen, look at me, and she looked up and saw in his eyes all he wanted to say like infinitesimal writing on coins and she grew still in herself and her eyes grew still and he said, Morgen, I want you to marry me. She shook her head and he said quickly, Why, Morgen?

You know I don't love you.

He pushed the glass out of the way and crossed his arms on the table and leaned closer to her over them. I know, Morgen, but you like to be with me or you wouldn't see me at all. I know you're like that about people. And that would be enough until you wanted it to change. He shook his head at the waiter and said, Later, and to Morgen said, I know right now lots of things're more important to you, your work, but I wouldn't get in your way, I swear I wouldn't, I wouldn't bother you at all. I love you and I can't bear being away from you so much. And you will change, Morgen, you've —

I don't think I want to change, Royal.

You will. You've got to. In the yellow light little beads of moisture came out on his forehead. He sat forward on his chair, his arms crossed on the table, the tablecloth wrinkled under his arms, his thin face growing thinner, marked all over with the sharp thumbprints of his love. Don't you see, he said, and the waiter came nearer again and made a sound in his throat and Royal turned his head angrily and said, Bring two more martinis, and to Morgen he said, I know you're not in love with me but that doesn't matter. I want to be near you all the time, that's all I want, just to be near you all the time.

Royal, she said, please don't let your —

Let me talk, he said. Her eyes were just as attentive but he knew it was slipping away from her. He saw it happen and he tightened himself all over as though he were bracing his whole body against the slipping weight of her body and he said, Oh, Morgen, if you knew, if you could just know. The waiter came with the cocktails and stood back a little and made that sound in his throat and Royal looked up and the waiter said, We close in half an hour, sir, and if you wish to order — but Royal, getting very thin and white around the mouth said, Will you get the hell away from here? and the waiter did, his shoulders lifted in disgust.

Royal, Morgen said.

He picked up his glass and drank. Well, good Lord! Morgen, let's go somewhere else where they don't bay at your elbow like a pack of hounds.

She rose immediately, leaving her glass untouched, and Royal tossed some money onto the table and took her arm. He got his hat and coat, keeping his left hand close around her arm, and they went out. In the street she looked up at him and he held her arm closer against his side and said, Where can we go? and, smiling not to wound him, she said, I think I'd rather go home.

He shook his head quickly. Tonight he wanted to keep her out of that house. We'll get a taxi, he said, and then we'll find a place. We're going to have dinner if I have to buy a restaurant.

No, Royal, I'd rather go home. I'll make supper for us and you can talk and I won't bay at your elbow.

He gave it up. All right. We'll get a taxi up at the corner.

In the taxi the meter started clicking and they moved out away from the curb and out of the light and Royal put his arm around her and said, Don't tell me not to do this, and she said nothing. She felt sorry about the evening and he put his face down against her hair and said, I love you so much I can't think of anything else to talk about, speaking very low and feeling her soft hair against his face and feeling her not really there but not caring now because she was there.

SHE lay awake, lonely in the night and the night haunted by the voices that seemed now to speak another language, the night sounds, a twig dropping, the surf sound of motor traffic in the streets somewhere below, and farther away a boat whistle now and then, all voices that had spoken to her out of the night for as long as she could remember and spoke now with words she didn't know. She lay very still, listening. Suddenly she felt a thin white terror of all she didn't know. With Fritz she lived in a world of knowing everything. They had given every sound a voice and a body but now everything was strange and she felt very awake and intent, as though some part of her were at the windows listening. She didn't know what had happened to her.

She turned her mind deliberately to Royal. An hour ago she had turned from him the moment she closed the door on the sound of his footsteps but now she took his face out of the dark and held it up in her mind and looked at it for a long time. It was a thin tight face with beautiful changing dark eyes but its mouth smiled too easily and too often. There was nothing in it for her, it didn't hold her and she allowed it to dissolve and in its place the other face appeared, the beautiful bearded face, the eyes bright blue like her eyes when she looked in a lighted mirror.

Gradually, so gradually she wasn't aware, the face she held became a mask and it slipped from her hands suddenly and she caught at it, her arms moved and she felt herself jerked violently out of the inner darkness of sleep.

Awake again she felt herself dividing, one part of her going toward the windows, the other lying awake on the bed. She rose and put on a woolen robe and went out through the dark house into the studio. She curled herself into one corner of the divan and after a long time saw the room change with light and saw herself change.

The package was small and trim. She went inside with it and crossed to the alcove and got the palette knife out of the drawer in Fritz's table. She cut the bands of paper tape and then held in her hands the long galley sheets of her book.

She went to the window seat and sat there looking idly at the first one, not reading but looking curiously at the words. They seemed strange, dissociated entirely from her. She wondered about that and didn't understand it. When Fritz completed a picture, after Mark set it in a frame, even after it was hung in a strange place, it still belonged to them.

The galleys didn't belong to her at all.

SHE went down the stairs carrying two cups and the coffeepot and Mark said, That's swell. Put it on the bench and I'll clear off a place for you to sit. He tightened the last clamp on the chair he was mending and stood up. There, he said, that'll hold her. He wiped his hands on his hip pockets and brought a high stool over to the work bench and dusted it off. Morgen got up on the stool and poured the coffee. Mark leaned against the bench and looked at the coffee steaming in the cups and then looked at Morgen, at her face and throat and shoulders and arms. You wouldn't know anything about it, he said, but two bits says you've gained a pound. He picked up both cups of coffee and gave her one. You're looking fine, Morgen. You're looking better all the time. It wasn't any good being off on a loose end like that, was it?

I still get lost, she said.

Sure, he said, nodding, who doesn't? That's one of the privileges of man. He stopped looking at her and began very softly to blow his coffee. He blew softly for a while, sending steam off in a thin sheet. I'm glad you're through with the galleys, he said. Now you can get busy and write a real book, not a fairy tale.

Childhood isn't a fairy tale, she said.

He laughed. Yours was.

Oh, Mark! She spilled coffee getting off the stool. Mark, what time is it?

He looked at the clock. It's there in plain sight, exactly four fifty-five.

I'll have to go, she said. Royal plays at five on the radio.

He caught her arm. Wait a minute. What's wrong with my radio?

All right, Mark, but hurry. Bring the coffeepot.

They went up the stairs, down a narrow corridor and out into a room walled on three sides with glass. Mark turned on the radio and they sat across the room from it on low wooden chairs placed side by side with their backs to the windows.

Morgen folded her legs under her. He's going to play some of his Telephone Pieces, she said. There's Transatlantic and No Answer and I can't remember the others but I think there were four. And an Erik Satie he said I'd like. I don't know Erik Satie, do you?

You won't even know yourself if you don't shut up, Mark said. Here. He gave her the cup of coffee she had forgotten and the announcer said, We regret to announce that Mr. St. Gabriel is ill and will be unable to play this afternoon. Morgen turned to Mark and the announcer said, We are looking forward to his return next week at the sa—

Mark turned off the radio and Morgen said, Why, Mark, he was all right last night.

He's probably all right now too, Mark said. He finished his coffee and set the cup down and began to search in all his pockets for cigarettes. Don't worry about it. All kinds of things could happen to a pianist, Morgen. He could cut his finger on a razor blade or something like that.

He was perfectly all right, Morgen said, frowning at her cup. He told me about his program for today and we talked. He was all right when he left.

He's all right, Mark said.

He took me to dinner and then talked so much and kept telling the waiter he'd order later and finally we had to leave without dinner. I was starved.

That's a fine kind of business, Mark said.

We came home and I made supper, she said. She looked down into her cup again and the line drew itself down between her brows. I wonder what could've happened to him.

LOOKING at his face it seemed to her that all its fine taut muscles had been clipped, allowing the flesh to sag. He looked different and at first it was difficult for her to talk to him. His eyes went moodily around the room, pausing, moving on. His right hand was discolored and swollen at the knuckles and there were slight abrasions stained red with mercurochrome. He looked very clean, as though he had been steamed and scrubbed. Even his clothes had a special look. He seemed thinner in his clothes.

I don't really remember much of it, he said slowly, but I remember what he said and how he looked when he said it. I didn't hit him hard enough to knock him out but he went down. It made me pretty sick. I got him up and Jimmy, that's the bartender, Jimmy got a cab and we got him into it and then I don't know where I went but I was in a steam bath this morning when I came around. That's all there was to it.

Morgen made a neat fold in the flannel over her thigh. It was so foolish of you to quarrel with Gildo, she said, the only friend that means anything to you.

Nobody means anything to me, he said. I don't want to be with anybody but you. I'm sick of people. When I'm not with you I don't want to talk to anyone, I don't want anyone else around me.

She said, Poor Royal, and slipped her hand under his arm and held her hand down along the inside of his wrist so that the tips of her fingers lay in the palm of his hand. His hand felt moist and soft and not like the hand she knew. I'm sorry, Royal. You don't know how sorry I am.

I don't want to know, he said. I don't want you to be sorry.

There's nothing else for me to be, Royal.

He moved his head and shoulders sharply and then folded his fingers up over the tips of her fingers. I wish you had a piano, Morgen. I wish I could say it to you that way. She was still against his arm and he recrossed his knees and said, I wish I could have my piano brought over here tomorrow. Then I wouldn't have to talk to you, I could say it all that way.

She said nothing and he too grew silent but they weren't together in silence and he knew this but he was too weary to struggle against it, too weary even to shut the thought out of his mind.

At two-thirty he rose, keeping her hand in his, and looked down at her with his weary eyes. Well, he said.

She pushed her free hand up through her hair. You've missed the last train, she said. You can stay here if you don't mind sleeping on the divan.

He went on looking at her, feeling her hand not there, feeling everything he wanted locked away behind the doors of her eyes.

I'm tired, Royal, and I know you are. I'll bring you some blankets.

He hadn't even said he'd stay, but he stayed and he lay awake smoking, throwing the cigarette ends one after another toward the black mouth of the fireplace. He lay awake for hours thinking about the way things had changed and shifted around him. He thought, I'm here, we're under the same roof, and then he began to wonder if his legs would take him across the dark studio to her door and through it. He knew they wouldn't because, thank God, he could still order his legs about, but he thought about it and the longer he thought about it the more he hated it, lying there alone and Morgen alone behind that door.

He stretched out his legs and put his heels up on the arm of the divan and gradually it died in him and he thought, Waiting's a hell of a lot easier than trying to forget you couldn't wait. And then he saw her eyes and the dark way they closed her within herself and he turned his head toward Fritz's door, but the back of the divan stood between it and his eyes, just as Fritz stood between what he wanted and what he couldn't have. He turned over on his side. What the hell was the matter with him, thinking such tripe? He threw away another cigarette and shut his eyes but he didn't sleep.

HE stood watching her measure the coffee into the basket. The fragrance of the coffee filled his nostrils. He rubbed his hand up across his face and said, I'm going to have my piano sent over today, Morgen.

She didn't look up. That would be very foolish.

Why foolish?

Why, because I'd have to have it sent right back.

He rubbed his unshaven cheek and then pushed his hands down into his pockets and turned away from her and looked out the open window onto the little terrace where he hung up the clothes that day. I was only kidding, he said. But I wish you'd let me have a phone installed, Morgen.

She put the coffee can back on the shelf. Oh, she said, I couldn't bear living with a telephone.

But nobody'd have to know about it but me.

It would be like living with an alarm clock that might go off any minute.

He put his hands on her shoulders and made her face him. Sometimes, he said, I think I could beat sense into you if I had the nerve to try. No piano, no phone, no

me, no nothing. He tried to laugh about it. You didn't
even say good morning to me.

I did, she said, but you didn't hear me. She reached
up and took hold of his wrists. Poor Royal, I believe you
struck matches all night.

Never mind, he said, letting his hands drop away from
her shoulders.

HE drank two cups of coffee and left, his face shadowed,
his long legs taking him slowly down the steps. His
subdued voice hung in the room like smoke after he
had gone. Morgen opened the windows and knelt on the
window seat and breathed the fresh bright air of morning.
How could she show him that the one he thought she was
lived only in himself? Going back across the room she saw
the littered hearth. She got the broom and swept the
cigarette ends and matches into the fireplace. These, she
thought, are all the letters he couldn't write to me. She
emptied ashtrays and moved pillows and rugs into their
usual places. She went to Fritz's door and opened it and
then sat down with her back to the sunlight, her body's
shadow shielding the typewriter.

THE moment he began to play everything else died in
her. She was enchanted and made to go where he chose
to take her. She was the note cut from crystal, she herself
was the crystal cut into notes of music. While he played
she wore herself like a necklace. She didn't know what
this enchantment was and afterward she never thought
about it, but she never missed the quarter hour that gave
it to her.

When he finished playing she went slowly to the
radio and turned it off and only the quiet of her own

house, whose quietness was close to her as her own heart, brought her back to herself.

She was sweeping the veranda when he called up to her from the road and she waved to him, leaning the broom handle against the railing and giving all her attention to him. He was carrying his coat and hat and in the sunlight his hair looked like some dark shining metal. He came up onto the veranda and dropped his coat over the railing and put his hat carefully on top of it. Stranger, he said, looking at her. She gave him her hands and he held them out and looked at her. He couldn't stop looking at her but he said lightly, Those dirty pants again. Don't you ever get them washed?

Oh, no, I like them this way.

You look so marvelous I could sing about it. Morgen, do you know how long it's been?

Days, she said.

Two weeks yesterday, he said. I counted them all the way to today. Today I had to stop counting. Have you missed me?

I've thought about you every day.

The hum died out of his ears. That isn't the same, he said, but I'll let it pass. I can't ever stay away so long again. He indicated the space separating them. May I come over there? She smiled and he took a step and put his arms around her and she stood quiet against him. You're like a statue that breathes, he said. I'll bet if I'd been carrying a suitcase you'd have said you didn't want any today, wouldn't you?

She crossed her arms between them, resting her elbows on his forearms. Oh, I think I'd have known you.

He smiled. Want to know another reason why I came over today? It's my birthday.

Oh, really?

He nodded. I thought we might have a party. A real

one. Both of us get tight as hatbands.

That would be fun, she said.

He pretended to have been hit in the face. It's all right, he said, laughing, only I was prepared to coax and wheedle and there I was with all those words in my mouth. Will you really go?

Of course.

After all my threats you still trust me like a brother?

She laughed and took herself out of his arms as though she were a magician. How old are you, Royal?

Sorry, he said, that's between me and my birth certificate. How's the new book coming along?

Nicely, thank you.

That's good. How about the other one?

It will be out before Christmas.

He turned her toward the open door and said, Let's give a copy to everybody we know at Christmas, shall we? They went inside and he lit two cigarettes and gave her one and looked around. What's different?

She looked. Why, nothing.

Something's different, he said. He looked all around the room carefully and finally discovered the change. The easel under the skylight was empty and the nude sleeping figure was gone. He thought about that for a moment and then said, I got a letter from Dad yesterday. He sat on the window seat and took the envelope out of his pocket.

Yes? she said.

He patted the cushion beside him. He sent some pictures. Come here. She sat beside him on the window seat and he gave her one of the pictures and said, This is looking from the main gate toward the beach.

It's lovely, she said.

This's Dad, he said, giving her another picture. The one with his pants rolled up. I don't know who the other fellow is. And this is Dad again. It's better of him.

She looked at the small brown face in the picture and said, You don't look like him at all, do you?

No, not much, Royal said.

She supposed he looked so dark because he was wearing white clothes. She couldn't associate him with Royal at all. He was small and burned black from the sun. She gave him the pictures and he put them in the envelope and put the envelope in his pocket. This was my annual bait letter, he said. I get one every year about this time. I always spend two weeks in the islands in January and Dad always writes me a month or two ahead. How'd you like to go home with me this year? I know you'd love it, you'd have a marvelous time.

We knew a painter once who lived in Honolulu, Morgen said. He died about five years ago.

How about it? Royal said, smiling. You could work there as easily as here and you'd have all that marvelous sun. Dad'd be crazy about you.

I don't know, Royal. It sounds very nice but I'd have to finish the book first.

A little fire burned up in his heart. Well, think about it anyway. It'd do you a lot of good. As for me, we'll skip that. Now let's talk about my birthday party.

THE night was blue all around them like a painted night. He stood with his hand through her arm, her cool ungloved hand locked in his. He didn't look at her face nor at her hand locked in his. She was everywhere, his eyes found her everywhere. At first, he said, I thought I ought to see an oculist, but after a while I realized it was simply a very special case of Morgen before my eyes. Now I'm used to it and it's wonderful.

She laughed and held her face down against his arm. This's the last party, she said, lifting her head and lifting back her hair carefully. Because when I drink that much everything I say is funny.

No, he said, when *I* drink that much everything I say is funny.

You don't understand, she said. She lifted her head and looked up into the deep center of the night, but she had to lower her head again. The glittering lights on the Berkeley hills swam about like thousands of tiny drunken fish, but she kept her eyes on them. Shall I tell you what I'm thinking, Royal?

He turned. Have you ever?

I'm thinking how dear you are to me because of all the things you've done that you didn't really have to do at all. I'm not saying it right, am I?

That's good enough for me. Go on.

No, that's all, Royal. She frowned and tried to remember exactly what she had wanted to say. It seemed so necessary to say it exactly but while she was thinking about it its importance escaped her, leaving her confused and not really there.

He felt it remotely and he unlocked his hand from hers and put his arms around her and bent his head until his chin rested on her bent head. My luck, he said. The sweetest part in the whole play and you forget your lines. How do you feel now?

All right, she said, but her mouth knew a flat taste and she was tired.

He lifted his head. I can't believe it now but we came up here to sober me up, didn't we? Come on, darling, our party's over. They walked a little way silently and then he said, In case you've forgotten, it was a hell of a swell party.

SHE unwrapped the books and took one to the window seat, just as she had taken the galleys, and she sat looking

at her face on the jacket and Morgen Teutenberg underneath and above that *The Island,* a first novel. Then she
was excited about it and she opened the book and read a
few words and turned a page and read again and it seemed
strange and wonderful to her now, the lines had a different
quality but they were hers and it was exciting. She closed
the book and looked at the dust jacket again. That was the
portrait Fritz liked best and in a way that made the book
a collaboration.

She couldn't sit there any longer. She wandered about,
carrying the book and looking at it. She looked at it all
over and then on the back flap of the jacket she read,
Morgen Teutenberg is the daughter of the late Fritz
Teutenberg, a distinguished American painter. We take
great pleasure in announcing that her biography of her
father is now in progress. The picture of Miss Teutenberg,
reproduced here, is one of a series of portraits he made
of her.

She went into Fritz's room and lay face down on his
bed, holding the book and holding in her throat a thick
weight of words. When the weight melted she cried a little
because of all the things she couldn't say to him.

SHE straighted her back and stretched her arms up over
her head. She thought of Mark, skiing at Yosemite. She
got up and turned on the radio and tuned in the first
sound she caught and let it beat against her ears. She went
to the window and looked out and went back to the divan
and looked down at the drawing board that held her work.
She had been drawing hands and mouths on the margins
of a page for half an hour. All four margins of the top
sheet were filled with badly drawn hands and mouths. She
went back across the room and turned off the radio. The
room's quiet held her for a moment and then she went to

the window again and knelt on the window seat and looked out. In the south there was pale winter sunlight that would die early. Evening would come, night would come. She wanted to lose herself in the deep forest of remembering backward into everything he had told her of his life, but she felt closed away from remembering. Somehow a gate had opened and closed and she was outside. I am like any other man, he told her once, but I want what I do to be different from what other men do.

She rose off her knees and went up into the alcove. She drew out the drawer in his table and moved things about, rearranging them without disturbing their order. She touched the brush handles with the tips of her fingers, rolling them back and forth. She took up one of his pipes and put it between her teeth. It was his working pipe, light, short in the shank. He could hold it in his teeth for hours without tiring his jaws. She stood there with the pipe in her mouth, looking down into the orderly table drawer. Finally she took the pipe out of her mouth and wiped the mouthpiece on her sleeve and put it back in the drawer. Everything he had done told its own story, everything told of his preoccupation with people, his indifference to place. That was simple enough.

She went back to the divan and looked at the page framed in mouths and hands. She read down the page and then, without thinking about it at all, she picked up her pencil and took another sheet and began to write very swiftly. The small swift writing went like a runner down the page, leaving its black footprints, leaping to another sheet, the handwriting no one else, not even Fritz, could decipher.

Someone knocked. She finished the sentence she was writing and went to the door and saw a telegraph boy, a small boy with reddened eyes and a running nose.

He reached toward his cap and said, Morgen Tooten-burg? She nodded and he said, Sign here.

She signed and took the telegram and he touched his nose with the back of his hand and said, I wasta wait for a nanser. Thanswer's prepaid.

She tore open the envelope and took out the message and read, PLEASE PLEASE MEET ME FERRY BUILD-ING FLOWERSTAND FIVE OCLOCK IMPORTANT ROYAL

She glanced at the boy and he touched his nose with the back of his small hand and she said, Just a moment, and took the blank inside and, leaning over the drawing board, she wrote, SORRY UNABLE TO COME MORGEN, printing the words carefully.

SHE knew, on her way to the door, that this time it was Royal and something in her paused though her feet took her on toward the door. It was Royal, smiling at her over a long florist's box.

Flowers, he said, for my favorite author.

She smiled and went backward into the room with the door.

And that isn't all, he said. He put the box on the window seat and reached into his topcoat pocket. I'm already on page one hundred and ninety-seven, Morgen, and it reads like a brook running fast and clear as crystal. He flushed a little up along his cheekbones and held out a copy of *The Island.*

She said, Thank you, Royal, and bent to open the box. She lifted out the flowers and they were lovely and cool and moist to her hands. She looked across them to Royal and said smiling, Delphiniums.

He stood, holding her book, looking at her holding his flowers. They're blue, he said.

She put them on the table in an old water pitcher and stood before them for a moment, rearranging, studying the effect. There, she said, and went and stood beside Royal at the hearth. She linked her forefingers behind her back and looked at him so long and so seriously he began to wonder. He shifted his weight onto one foot and she said, I've never told you not to bring gifts, have I? I mean flowers and the radio — I was wondering just now if it would have made a difference if I had told you not to do things like that.

He laughed, relieved and really amused. Don't you want to know why I wanted you to come over this afternoon?

Yes.

He stepped back and drew her back to the divan. A marvelous thing happened, he said, settling his shoulders against the cushion. Have you ever been walking along the street and suddenly for no apparent reason felt as though you'd walked into a wall in the dark? That's what happened to me. Mind you, I wasn't looking to the right or left, just walking along. Then I hit this wall in my consciousness and I stopped and when I turned my head there you were! I stood there so long it's a wonder they didn't call a cop to chase me off. Then I had an inspiration and sent you the wire. I didn't believe for a minute you wouldn't come. He smiled into the fire. There's a poster same as this, he touched the book jacket, about the size of the original I imagine, and a copy of the book opened to the dedication, and three more books. The whole window's perfect. Wait'll you see it.

She dropped her head back against the cushion and laughed, the lovely laughter he loved and almost never heard. Oh, Royal, she said, you're the sweetest person.

He felt the words go down into him like arrows finding a warm unprotected heart, but he had learned, he
only smiled and settled himself deeper against the back
cushion. Do you know what I'm going to do some day?
I'm going to buy up every portrait he made of you, Morgen. He looked at her face on the book jacket for a
moment and then he lifted himself slightly and took his
fountain pen out of his vest pocket. Smiling, saying
nothing, he gave her the book and the fountain pen.

SHE set the candle on the windowledge above the crèche.
The candle flame against the window made two lights.
She lifted her eyes slowly and looked at her reflection,
bright above the mirrored light of the candle, and saw
the other face.

Royal, putting the lights on the little tree, paused
and said smiling, You can give me a hand, here, Nar-
cissus.

She shook her head in a sudden sharp bitterness and
he came up behind her and she lowered her eyes to the
crèche, not to see his image on the window. Before he
could speak she said, When I was six he let me think I
helped make the crèche. We've always put it at the window
and the candle above like this.

I know, he said.

She knew he didn't know. He was beside her but
Fritz was all around her like warm stifling air and in
despair she turned and put her arms around Royal and
she saw the evening like the colors in a kaleidoscope,
the children's songs she sang in German, the marzipan,
the kirsch, the little gold-dusted tree with blue lights,
the crèche, the candle on the windowledge, all of it
meaningless, all of it bitter in her mouth like laughter.
She began to laugh this bitterness against Royal's arm,

softly and bitterly because of the Christmas eve, because it would never mean anything again, because it was Royal who was there with her.

He stood, afraid to move but moved speechless within, until she lifted her head. She looked drunk in the eyes. She looked at him and wondered what he would say if he knew and she laughed again.

Morgen, he said.

Finish the tree, she said. Is it finished?

Just a couple more lights, he said. He didn't know what had happened to her but he went back to the tree, wearing the memory of her body against his like a thin hot suit of armor. He began to thread the last two lights out along the branches.

Morgen sat on the divan and poured another little glass of kirsch and drank it and it was more bitterly sweet now, and she said, Then turn off the other lights, Royal.

He said, Just a tick, and turned the switch and the little tree grew up, bright with its small blue lights. He whistled. Look, Morgen!

She turned and looked not at the tree but at Royal and he went about turning out the lamps and then he sat beside her in the firelight and said, I'll bet we're the only two kids in the world up this late on Christmas eve. Then, aware of her eyes, aware of the unbelievable thing they said, he looked at her fully and he couldn't believe she was looking at him like that but his heart knew it and began to pound in his ears and he said, Darling. Hesitating and not sure of himself he put his arms around her. Oh, darling, darling. He kept saying that, he couldn't say anything else. He kissed her and at first her mouth was warm and soft and like a child's mouth and he said, Oh, Morgen, and kissed her again but differently and no one had ever kissed her that way and she hated it. Oh, Morgen, he said.

I want to stay with you, Morgen let me stay, and she said, Yes, I want you to.

SHE was fiercely glad for the dark in her room because he was a naked stranger and she couldn't have looked at him, she couldn't have made herself look at him. When her eyes grew accustomed to the dark she closed them tightly and turned her head toward the wall and then her teeth grew together with pain and disgust but mostly pain. It was no more than that.

When he slept she lifted herself a little but his shoulders and his head between her breasts held her there like a stone. She lay looking over his head toward the open door in shame and sadness.

The tiny blue lights burned on the tree, but coldly now in the gray light of morning.

WHEN she woke her shoulders and arms were bare and cold and Royal's head had slipped away from her body. She looked down at his head and began to tremble. She clenched her teeth but the trembling shook her and Royal stirred and opened his eyes.

He lifted himself slowly onto his elbows and slipped his hands under and around her. She looked at him. He, in wonder, found her there and wonder kept him wordless. Then tears filled his eyes, his eyes got very bright from within and he kissed her, her mouth gently, her eyelids, her temples, her throat. I can't believe I'm here, he said.

She looked at him with her dark unhappy eyes and said, I can.

He drew back a little to look at her. Morgen, you're not happy.

She couldn't bear to look at his eyes. She drew his head down and held it with her hands gentle and she saw him close his eyes. For a while he breathed like a man asleep and then he said, You'll be stung in a thousand places, darling, and smiled. I hope you've got a razor. Suddenly he held his head closer to her than her hands held it. Morgen, I can't believe this. I can't.

Her eyes wandered over him. You're so thin, Royal. I didn't know how thin you were.

He lifted his head and kissed the point of her chin. I know. My tailor attends to the deception. I'd better start getting this beard off, darling. You come too. He started to rise and then hesitated. Darling, are you all right?

No, she said.

He moved over to the edge of the bed and sat up. He rubbed his hand up along his lean arm to the shoulder and down again to the wrist. I don't know why it has to be the way it is with a girl, he said slowly. He closed his fingers and felt the hard tendons of his wrist and stood up. He looked taller and thinner without clothes. His body was like a thin piece of metal, the muscles showing sharply. He said, Well, I'll — Good Lord, we left the tree lights on!

I know, Morgen said.

SHE had never watched a man shave. She stood in the corner beyond the washbowl and watched him lather his face with her soap and shave with her razor. She lit a cigarette and they smoked it together. On another day, she thought, it would have amused her. She looked away from his face in the mirror. The bathroom was small and compact, painted smoky gray with scarlet details. She had always thought it was the nicest room in the house. When you stood facing the mirror over the washbowl, your head was a portrait painted on the scarlet shower curtain. The curtain was dark now, damp from her shower.

When Royal finished shaving he drank from her water glass and she looked up at him and saw his teeth through the glass and thought they looked like a horse's teeth polished white.

AT the door he put his arms around her and said, I hate not being with you on Christmas, darling, but I'm already on my way back tomorrow. She saw his eyes begin to light within and she waited as though she were waiting for him to strike her. Morgen, he said, it takes three days to get married. Can't we start getting married tomorrow? He tightened his hands on her arms and held her away from him. Then in two weeks we could sail for the islands. Oh, Morgen, I've thought of it a thousand times but I never let myself believe we'd really go together, I mean the two of us written like one person. Mr. and Mrs. Royal St. Gabriel. Hasn't that a marvelous sound, Morgen?

She only looked at him.

Poor darling, he said. Poor sweet. Morgen, I love every moment you've ever given me, none more than the rest. You know that, don't you?

I know, she said.

After today I'll never say good-bye again, he said. He kissed her and opened the door. I'll be over early in the morning. Be happy, darling.

She closed the door on the way his eyes held reaching to her eyes and went first to the tree and turned off its lights and then she went to the crèche and looked down at it without tenderness. She packed away the little figures but left the box there on the windowledge. All her movements were slow and uncertain as though she had walked ahead into time and found old age too soon. She went to the fireplace and put wood on the fire and then sat on the hearth and bent forward over her knees and thought, If he knew he'd jump off the boat into the bay. She put her head on her knees and looked at the firelight moving lightly on the wall and thought, Now I'm not that one, I'm another now.

SHE went slowly up the steps, tired from walking so far, her mind tired from holding the one thought too long. She didn't know how to tell him it had been like watching herself die and that she had known it would be like that. She wished something would prevent his coming today.

The door opened away from her hand before she touched it and he stood there in the doorway. He took both her hands and began slowly to break their bones. Good Lord, Morgen, you scared me to death! Where've you been? I've been waiting an hour.

She drew her hands out of his and looked at him with nothing in her eyes. Don't ever say where've you been like that to me, she said. Her voice was like ice over moving water. No one, no one in the world has the right to ask me where I've been.

He clamped his hand around his wrist. Why, you know I didn't mean anything. I've been waiting so long I got nervous, that's all. I'm sorry I spoke that way, Morgen. Here, give me your coat. Come get warm. You must've been gone for hours. The house was like an icebox when I got here.

She let him take her coat and went slowly away from him to the fire and stood very straight and tall at the hearth and held out her cold hands to its warmth. She began to speak before he reached her. No one has ever spoken to me that way, she said. No one.

He turned her about sharply. I told you I was sorry, didn't I? What's the matter with you?

She looked at him out of her clear cold eyes. My conscience, she said in the same clear way. I've never done a thing I was ashamed to think about. I did a terrible thing last night, Royal. Last night I got terribly lost. I couldn't bear the Christmas eve alone, it didn't mean anything and I had to forget that it didn't and you were here.

Unconsciously his lips parted a little away from his white teeth as though they were being lifted carefully on small hooks. Then it's true, he said, taking his hands off her shoulders, what Gildo said was true.

I don't know what Gildo said. What I said was true.

He stood with his hands hanging. He felt himself going heavy and out of this heaviness he said, I could kill him. He saw Fritz's face as he'd seen it that day and he said slowly, I wish I'd done it, I wish I'd choked him black in the face like that. I'd have something to be grateful for.

She was looking at him with her eyes getting stiller and darker and suddenly she covered her ears with her hands and went past him into her room.

He heard the door close and he stood there with his stomach contracted, his arms trembling, his whole body beginning to tremble. The fire crackled and spat out a live coal and without thinking he set his foot on it and then he thought his legs weren't going to hold him up any longer and he moved backward to the divan and sat down. He lit a cigarette with his hands shaking so much he had to use both hands. He inhaled deeply and blew smoke out and watched it fog the air against the firelight. What had he done? He leaned forward and put his elbows on his knees and looked at his shaking hands. My God, what had he done? He threw the cigarette into the fire and ran his forefinger around inside his collar. He ran his hands back over his hair and rose suddenly and went to her door. Morgen, he said. There was no answering sound. Morgen, he said. He tried the door and it wasn't locked. He opened it and saw her lying face downward on the bed, her head held in her hands. He knelt beside the bed and took one of her hands away from her face. He didn't speak for a long time. Morgen didn't move.

I never saw anybody cry like that, he said finally, with never any tears. He opened her hand gently and laid his face on it. I've never seen anyone like you, I've never loved anyone but you. I can't ever stop loving you, Morgen, no matter what you do or I do I can't stop. You're in me like my own flesh and bone. His tears ran warm down across his cheekbone and into her hand. I didn't mean what I said, Morgen, I didn't mean any of it. Do you hear? I just hit back. Morgen listen to me. I know today wasn't happy for you. Maybe I shouldn't have come at all but I want you to know I love you and that I didn't mean what I said. I won't go till you tell me you know I didn't mean it.

He lifted his head and looked at her and he saw in her face what he wanted to see. He kissed her wet palm and stood up. Her eyes didn't follow him. He went out, wiping his face with his handkerchief, and got his hat and coat and went out the door and down the steps.

At the first house down the hill he rang the doorbell and without looking at the woman who opened the door he said, I beg your pardon. If you have a telephone I'd like to call a taxi. I'm not feeling well.

SHE lifted Isolde onto the drainboard and looked into her

ears and examined her coat carefully. You've been away
so long, she said softly, and I didn't even miss you. Well,
you're clean as a pin. Wherever you go you always remember your beautiful coat, don't you?

Isolde stretched out her forepaws, showing her claws
and hiding them again. She stretched leisurely all over
and then she leapt lightly to the floor and went off to her
place on the window seat in the studio.

Morgen followed smiling. She sat beside Isolde on
the window seat. She drew her knees up and locked them
in her arms. Isolde interrupted her purring to yawn, showing all her small white pointed teeth. Morgen felt as though
she too were purring. It seemed like the first day of a new
year. She felt new. Like the earth must feel, she thought,
when the grass is up on the hills and down among the roots
of trees and grass it's suddenly spring.

AND Royal too was up early, but with an aching head and
his thoughts tangled. He walked aimlessly around the room
drinking black coffee. He was careful how he walked and
turned, not to set his head rattling apart again. In the
night, in one of those cool crystal pauses in the descent to
unconsciousness he saw everything as it really was. He was
in a taxi going from one place to the next and with the
windows down and the night cool on his face he knew it
was all his fault because he hadn't given her time to adjust
herself to living separated from her father. Things like
that came slowly and he had hurried her out of it too
soon. He knew how close she had always been to her
father and maybe he had tried too late to change that, to
separate her from himself, but it hadn't been the other
thing. He knew that. He didn't know how he'd got insane
and let himself forget for a moment that he knew. She had
come first to him. If her heart had been enclosed in her

father's heart all her life that was all right, it was a perfectly natural thing. She hadn't known her mother at all. Good Lord, she hadn't even had children to play with when she was a child. She hadn't gone to school a day in her life. So far as he knew she'd never had any friends, except of course her father and friends of his, old men probably. That fellow who lived up on the hill above her was probably the only other fellow, anywhere near her own age, she'd ever known.

Well, he had it all straightened out. He wished he'd come home instead of going on to another place. He could have written her a letter out of the clear way his thoughts had arranged themselves. But he hadn't come home and now his head ached and threatened to fly into bits whenever he moved it and he knew he couldn't write.

He sat at the piano, sipping his black coffee. On the rack he saw a note he had made on the back of an envelope. He read Yerba Buena 1 the little white flowers 2 the coming 3 siesta. He set his coffee on the bench and concentrated his thoughts on the words. Somewhere, waiting to see someone, he'd picked up a book on early California. He couldn't remember it clearly but he had heard something, something had sung to him out of the pages and he had seen a ballet coming out of it.

He stared at the words and under his eyes the words went away and the warmth of his heart began to spread outward over his body like tender hands. He would go somewhere, not home yet, he'd go somewhere and work on the ballet and then when he came back he'd go to Morgen and show her his clean slate and say, Now let's start all over.

He telephoned a telegram to her and then took a shower, the water running tepid at first and hardening gradually into cold. While he was drying his back he decided where he would go.

HERE, he said, reaching his hand down to her.

She came up onto the wall beside him, using his foot and hand for a ladder.

Well, he said, how's everything? You a best seller yet? Oh, no.

He motioned back over his shoulder with his thumb. People moving in up there, did you notice?

Oh, really? She looked up at the little house. It looked just the same.

How's your pianist?

Royal? He's away writing a ballet. Was the skiing good?

I don't know, he said. Oh, sure, it was swell.

You're burned a lovely color, like a baked apple. And why did you get your hair cut so short?

He ran his hand up over his head. I don't know.

She moved a little away from him on the wall. Mark, are you troubled about something?

He swung his heels against the wall and then looked at her and stopped swinging his heels. While I was away, he said, I fell in love with a girl and it's got me by the ears.

Oh, she said.

Well, don't look superior. Why shouldn't I fall in love if I want to?

She moved farther away, lifted her feet and stretched them out away from him and lay flat on her back with her head near his hand. Because you don't look happy about it, she said. You ought to look awfully happy.

I am happy, he said. It's not the kind of happiness you go around telling people about, that's all.

You don't sound like Mark at all, she said. She put her hands under her head and lay looking at the sky. I don't think anyone in love is ever really as happy as he thinks he is, Mark. It's always either the remembrance of happiness or anticipation of it.

And you don't know a damned thing about it, he said, looking down at her. She closed her eyes and he looked at her pointed face serene in the light, at the softened points of her breasts under the knit shirt, the arch of her ribs, her sunken body, the long slim thighs. A strand of her hair lay against his hand like a cobweb. Looking down at her he began to smile but unexpectedly the stillness of her face bit at him with sharp teeth. He looked away from her. You've been raising hell while I was gone, he said. You look like a piece of spaghetti. You probably haven't had a decent meal or a full night's sleep for God knows how long. I don't know what's the matter with you. You go along fine as a new dollar for a while and then all of a sudden — Abruptly he felt alone on the wall and he looked down as though he had expected to find her dissolved into the air and invisible. He moistened his dry roughened lips and said softly, Morgen?

She was asleep.

THE door was open. She glanced in and knocked lightly on the door and it swung back a little. No one came and she knocked again. Well, people didn't go altogether away and leave their doors wide open. She looked inside deliberately then. She didn't see a telephone but she was pleased with what she did see. It was a room bent low over itself and over what it held. She wondered if the same people still lived there. She remembered them, the old man with the pointed white beard and the girl, very slim and tall and quiet. She even remembered her name, but not her last name. She looked all around and then pushed her hands down into her pockets and walked back across the veranda and down the steps. She liked houses built along hillsides. She turned to follow the flagstones around the corner of the house and then, glancing up, she saw Morgen flat on the wall like a bright lizard in the sun and she stopped. She knew Morgen instantly. She stood still for a moment and then went forward slowly, going as near as she could without stepping up on the terrace.

Morgen heard a step and without opening her eyes she smiled and said, I'm awake, Mark. She waited and then turned her head and opened her eyes. Oh, she said and sat up. The girl looked up at her with dark uninquisitive eyes and the gentlest smile Morgen had ever seen. Then she knew the face and she went back a long way and found the name. Why, she said, you're Toni.

The gentle smile deepened. And you're Morgen.

Morgen dropped her feet over the wall and dusted her hands slowly one against the other. Then it's you who're moving into the little house.

My aunt and I, Toni said.

I can't imagine how you remembered my name, Morgen said. I can't imagine how I remembered yours. She sat looking down into that odd penetrating gentleness of Toni's eyes. And now, she said smiling, you're going to live here again.

Toni nodded, watching Morgen come down off the wall and come toward her. I wondered if you still lived here, she said. I remember the way you and your father —

He died five months ago, Morgen said.

Toni said, Oh, I'm sorry, and the smile left her eyes. She looked up toward the place on the wall Morgen had occupied and looked beyond it, upward through the trees to her own house. She thought of the thing that had happened there long ago, a horrible thing without reality now. I came down, she said, to ask if I could use your telephone. We've been waiting all afternoon for the water to be turned on.

82

I haven't a telephone, Morgen said. Did you try at that house?

Toni nodded. Yes, but no one answered. Some machine was making a dreadful noise but no one answered the door.

Morgen laughed. That's a lathe. Mark Strauss lives there. She pushed her hair upward and back and held the ends in one hand. I'll go up with you and show you where the telephone is.

Toni turned suddenly and looked down. Oh, she said, what a handsome fellow.

That handsome fellow, Morgen said smiling, is Isolde.

Toni knelt and held out her hand. Isolde touched it lightly with her nose and then with her shoulder. What a lovely hospitable creature, Toni said. Morgen smiled, looking down at Toni's head. It was a beautiful head, tapering smoothly into the neck, the neck joining the shoulders in clean strong lines. She glanced up smiling and rose, holding Isolde. I'd like to kidnap her, she said.

Morgen let the ends of her hair fall. That won't be necessary, she said. Within a week you'll be thinking of ways to get rid of her. She's an inveterate caller.

Toni lifted Isolde's head and looked gravely into her eyes. I can't think of anything nicer, she said. She played with one of Isolde's ears for a moment and then she said, Well, I really should attend to my call.

Yes, Morgen said. There's a path up the hill there but we'll have to climb the wall.

Toni bent and opened her arms and Isolde left them. Morgen started back along the house and Toni followed and they went up across the terrace and climbed the wall. This was the Rubicon I never crossed, Toni said, looking back at the wall.

I asked you to, Morgen said, smiling. Several times I think.

But I never dared.

Morgen went ahead up the hill. In her mind she began to wind the moment with fine soft threads. She stooped and picked up a fallen eucalyptus branch and stripped it of its leaves.

Toni looked back down the hill and saw Isolde sitting in the exact center of a flagstone, watching them. She smiled and looked ahead again. This house wasn't here, she said.

No, Morgen said. Mark built it four years ago. We used to have this slope to ourselves but it's almost built in now.

Yes, Toni said, it's changed.

Mark saw them through the window and cut the power on the lathe and Morgen waved to him with the branch she carried. They went around the corner of the house and he came to the shop door and said, You walking in your sleep again? He was powdered all over with fine wood dust.

Morgen smiled and glanced back at Toni. Toni, this is Mark Strauss. She's going to live next door to you, Mark, and she wants to use your telephone.

Mark nodded to the girl. Sure, he said. You show her, Morgen. I don't want to go upstairs till I'm through. I cleaned house this morning. He smiled and brushed dust from his eyebrows. The door's open.

Toni said, Thank you very much, and followed Morgen on around the house. They went into the entry and Morgen showed her the telephone and then went back outside again and waited, leaning against the house. She heard Toni's soft voice and she paused over it and listened to its texture and she thought she had never heard a lovelier voice. She tossed away the branch and looked out over the bay to the sky deepening behind clouds lined with flame. Watching it was like looking at a page in a book she hadn't seen since childhood.

I WAS closing the windows and I heard what I thought was somebody trying the pitch on a kettledrum and I thought that was funny but I didn't pay much attention. I don't know how long it took me to realize the sounds were words, meant for me. Anyway I leaned out and there was this woman. Young man, she said, would you be so good as to come up here with an ax or whatever is necessary to get water running in my house? Laughter choked him. He leaned back and laughed until his eyes were wet.

Morgen pressed her teeth into an olive. When he could hear her she said, Did you get the water turned on?

Oh, sure, he said. He shook his head and speared slices of ham and slices of cheese and filled his plate again.

The man didn't come, after all, Morgen said.

Mark shook his head. Boy, she was a picture! Big as a house, helpless as a mouse, puffing away on the blackest cigar you ever laid eyes on. He wiped the corners of his eyes with his napkin. She took a fancy to the size of my chest. Asked me if I was a singer. She's a singing coach or something. The girl treats her like the Queen of Sheba.

Morgen looked at the mark her teeth had made in the olive. Well, I'm glad you could turn on the water for them.

Boy, he said, I wonder what I'm in for.

Why?

Oh, that voice of hers and people vocalizing.

All you have to do is start your lathe, Morgen said, smiling.

He grunted. You can't run it twenty-four hours a day. He glanced at her empty plate. Come on, he said, eat something.

I've been eating all the time, she said. You were too busy laughing to see.

Well, have some more beer.

No, thank you, she said. I'll have coffee when you're ready.

He looked at her. By the way, how come you're having supper with me?

She decided to eat the olive. I don't know, she said. I didn't want to be alone, I guess.

He nodded and went on eating ham and cheese and bread, the slices of ham and cheese rolled neatly around his fork, the bread in big thickly buttered bites from a slice as thick as his hand.

SHE came out of a deep sleep, the waking clean as a sharp knifecut. There was fog, she felt it first and then saw it in the air when she reached to get a cigarette. She covered herself quickly again, all but her right arm, and smoked and thought about the day lying unknown like a mountain path before her. She thought about Toni, she thought about herself seen through Toni's eyes. She even thought about Royal, tenderly and briefly. She knew now that the disgust that had been in her like death in this room was lost somewhere in the secret places of sleep and she would never know it again. She dropped ashes on the blanket and blew them gently off onto the floor. A foghorn was sounding somewhere, alone and lost in the gray morning. For years she thought foghorns were Cyclopes snoring in their sleep. She held Fritz close to her for a while and then she snuffed out her cigarette and drew her bare arm in under the covers. The day, its whole unknown length and breadth, stretched out before her again.

MORGEN set the wood basket down and locked the door and turning to pick up the basket again she saw Toni looking down at her from above, very brown in her blue clothes. She smiled and lifted her hand and Morgen smiled.

Good morning, they said.

HE closed the book and leaned back in his chair and laced his hands across his tight vest. Now, he said. The telephone rang and he grunted and unclasped his hands and brought the telephone to the edge of the desk. Excuse me, he said, keeping his eyes on Morgen. Yes? Oh, all right. Tell him I'll meet him there at three. He replaced the telephone and leaned back again. Now, young lady, he said, I've finished with you professionally. I can't say to you this is wise or that is unwise. I can say find out the difference between the real and the false. You'll have to rely on your instinct and I know it's perfectly reliable because you're a sensible girl, always have been. You proved it today by coming to me.

They smiled at each other and Morgen rose. I'm glad I came.

He rose slowly and went around the end of the desk and put his arm around her shoulders. I'm glad too, he said, very glad. He went with her toward the door. If you're not engaged tomorrow night, he said, I might remind you that Thursday's still Hassenpfeffer night at my house.

Thank you, Morgen said. She leaned and kissed his cheek. I remember. I won't be able to come tomorrow but I'll come soon. Goodbye, Dr. Stauber.

Good-bye, my dear. He held open the door for her and watched her cross the room and then closed the door. He sighed and patted the big bulge of his stomach. Once when she was still a little sliver of a girl she put her hand flat on his diaphragm and said, Will you please laugh again? He let himself down into his chair and, glancing at the clock, rubbed his hands forward over his thick short white hair. The loneliness of grief did extraordinary things to people sometimes. How old was she? Twenty-one. Old enough to know a thing for itself. A fine beautifully made girl. He pulled his engagement pad toward him. He thought a little of those fine beautiful children he'd always planned on her producing. Well, if he'd got children himself he might not have been so anxious to stand godfather to someone else's. He picked up the telephone.

TONI was wearing the faded blue slacks and a jacket too short in the cuffs, and her face and hands and ankles were smooth and brown in the sunlight. She looked at the water spread like a great shining carpet below them and said, It was lovely to wake and see the fog but it's lovelier to see it lift and thin against the sun.

It's loveliest at evening, Morgen said.

Toni's hands were brown as leaves against Isolde's golden coat. She's almost the color of your hair, Toni said.

Morgen smiled. My father used to say he often kissed her good night by mistake. But that couldn't have been true because she never slept on my bed, even when she was a kitten.

Isolde moved her tail indolently and Toni looked at it and said, You've lived here all this time?

For ten years, Morgen said.

We came after you. I must have been eight or nine because I've been away eight years and I'll soon be seventeen.

Do you remember how you used to stand up there and never move and never say a word?

Toni nodded smiling. I remember the first time you asked me to come down. You and your father were digging something there where the terrace is now.

Morgen laughed. It was a fish pond. I'd forgotten about it completely.

I wasn't sure I wanted to come back, Toni said. I didn't remember it the way it really is, the hills green like they are now and the bay and the air so clean to breathe. Now I know I'm glad we came.

Morgen locked her arms around her knees. I know, she said. I knew yesterday when I looked down and saw you looking at *me*. That would have been in me always, even if I'd never seen you again.

Toni looked down at Isolde again. Gentleness like dark mist gathered in her eyes. She began to speak, but very softly, as though they were in a crowded room. They were sitting on the wall and the whole morning began to radiate from the place they occupied.

FINALLY she left the window and got her coat and went out into the rain. She walked up around the hill, past Mark's gate, up the three steps to Toni's door. She knocked and waited and then knocked again. After waiting a long time, unprotected from the rain, she went down the steps and around the house to the double doors on the side. The doors were glass-paned and uncurtained and she looked in and saw an enormous woman sitting in a peel chair with her small feet in heelless slippers. Her head was tipped back and her nose was hidden in a glass. Morgen tapped on the door and saw the nose emerge from the glass slowly and with a lovely dignity. Their eyes looked at each other through the crosshatch of rain on the glass and Morgen smiled. The woman beckoned and Morgen opened the door and stepped inside. She said, You're Toni's Aunt Lida, aren't —

Oh, I know who you are, Aunt Lida said, smiling. My dear, you're the image of your handsome father.

Morgen looked at her. Did you know my father?

A very handsome man. She swept the air with her fat dark hand. A glass of sherry, my dear? An excellent lubricant for the throat. I recommend it highly. Toni!

Oh, Toni's out. Salvador! She set her glass beside the carafe on the table at her elbow and clapped her fat hands. Salvador! Where's that boy? Where's my bell?

Morgen stood motionless at the door. Is Toni here?

Toni? Aunt Lida felt carefully all over the high dark arrangement of her hair, felt the small gold rings at her ears. Toni, let me see, I believe Toni went to San Francisco this morning. No, forgive me, that's tomorrow, isn't it? She saw Morgen standing at the door. My dear, won't you sit down? That chair is very comfortable, though you're tall and it might be rather low for you. Will you have a glass of sherry, my dear?

Morgen smiled politely and shook her head. No, thank you, she said, I must go. Will you tell Toni I was here?

Certainly, Aunt Lida said. Toni ran down to the lending library to exchange some books for me. She should be back directly.

Morgen drew a deep breath and opened the door. She said, Good-bye, without looking back and heard the deep voice say, Such nasty weather, so —

She went around the house with her head bent to the rain and wind. She hesitated at Mark's gate but she went on, thinking that Toni might have stopped in on her way home.

Toni wasn't there. She looked at the room's emptiness for a moment and then she laughed and put wood on the fire and took off her wet coat and hung it in the bathroom on the shower rod. She dried her wet hair and brushed it. In the mirror she was another person with her smooth darkened hair.

SHE sat low on the divan with her shoulders and neck bent sharply against the back cushion. The wind roared in the chimney and the acacias beat against the house under the windows. If you sit like that, Fritz used to say to her, you'll grow into a concertina. She lifted herself a little. She had been looking into the fire so long her eyes ached with looking. Darkness knelt in the room, though it was still the time before sunset. The rain came in spasms, beating at the windows with small vicious knuckles. She was waiting but when she heard the other knocking it was in her ears only a variation of the same theme and she didn't move. Then it came again and this time the sound penetrated and she went swiftly to the door and opened it.

She stood silent and without moving for so long Toni finally laughed and stepped inside unasked. She took Morgen's hand off the door and closed it herself.

When you laugh like that, Morgen said, you're all silver and crystal.

Toni laughed again and began to unfasten her raincoat.

Let me help you, Morgen said. Oh, you're so wet! You're getting wet.

There, Morgen said. Let me take it.

I might have taken my gloves off first, Toni said, smiling.

Morgen looked at her hands coming out of the wet gloves. I thought you'd never come, Toni. I went up to your house.

Aunt Lida told me. I meant to come earlier but I didn't know I was going to the library.

They smiled at each other and Morgen took the dripping coat and hung it beside hers in the bathroom and Toni made cautious footsteps across the floor to the hearth. Morgen came back with a bathtowel and a pair of straw scuffs. Toni smiled at them and sat on the divan and unbuckled her small thick-soled shoes and Morgen, sitting on the hearth, took them one after another out of her hands and put them to dry. Toni slipped her bare brown feet into the scuffs and Morgen gave her the towel and, smiling, still saying nothing, she sopped her short hair and then, letting the towel drop onto her shoulders, looking like a child just out of its bath, she leaned forward and said, Brunnehilde circled with fire.

A stillness went around them and Morgen leaned across this stillness to touch the hands and face she loved. That was a moment made wholly of tenderness. She withdrew from it gently, sitting erect again but not alone. You're so known to me, she said slowly. It isn't possible for one person suddenly to be everything like this, but you are. Her voice sank and she smiled and after a moment she said, I was waiting. I didn't know what I was waiting for, I didn't even know I was waiting, but when I saw you I knew.

HER money's almost gone, though of course she doesn't know that, but it was the threat of war as much as anything else. I know she's as tired as I am of living in pensions and railroad sleeping cars. I didn't know whether the house was vacant or not but I cabled the agent. I didn't tell Aunt Lida until it was all arranged.

When you left here, Morgen said, did you go to live with her?

Not at first. She selected a school for me and she went on selecting schools until I was fifteen. Of course I spent my summers with her but I got awfully tired of that.

Toni, will she be disturbed if you stay?

No, Toni said. She's asleep by now. Salvador sleeps in a cubby at the end of the hall and he can hear if she calls.

This afternoon when I was there, she spoke as though she'd known my father.

Toni laughed. When Mr. Strauss was up that first evening he said you were the daughter of Fritz Teutenberg and he said it in a way that told us we knew nothing at all if we didn't know about Fritz Teutenberg. She turned her head in the arm that framed it. I'm afraid Aunt Lida gave Mr. Strauss a bad moment. She told him she was a voice coach.

But isn't she?

She hasn't coached for years. She mixes everything up, Morgen. Poor old fellow. She's been ill for a long time and it doesn't really matter much what she does. It's my business to see that she's happy.

Morgen said nothing but after a moment she reached out into the firelight and touched that last word gently.

SHE knew when Toni left her. She lifted herself a little and thought, In sleep you seem almost not to breathe. Where do you go? and then her thoughts became formless and liquid. She lay separate and awake, looking at the silhouette of Toni's head on the pillow. She heard the campanile chime three o'clock. The sound of the wind and rain had softened into silence but the darkness had a voice and it spoke insistently. Finally she said, Toni?

Toni turned her head. Yes?

I had to say your name.

My heart and I are sleeping, Toni said.

You did sleep a little, Toni. I watched you.

With cat's eyes, Toni said smiling. You say my name as if you'd given it to me.

There's no other way to say it.

Didn't you sleep, Morgen?

No, Morgen said. She felt Toni slipping away from her again into sleep. She lay listening with her fingertips and heard the heart slow and the soft beating go deep and then without warning breath and pulse and nerves caught and turned in her and she turned.

She woke Toni again but so gently waking was like dreaming.

WHEN Toni opened her eyes she saw a strange room bright with light. She lay in space touching nothing. Then she turned slightly, finding herself, and her ankles moved against Morgen's. In sleep they had drawn apart all but their ankles. She turned her head and saw Morgen's hair on the pillow and she saw her face, pale with soft fringed shadows under the eyes, her long curved throat. She held her breath. She wanted to melt and pour herself around Morgen like wax.

AND when Morgen opened her eyes they clouded with a startled darkness at first and then Toni smiled and said, Don't look at me like that. It makes me feel like an impostor, and then Morgen too smiled and they looked at each other and went back into the night and brought the two they were into the bright tender quietness of the morning.

Your eyes are dark underneath.

I was dreaming, Morgen said. You were driving two little wedges into my eyes with a golden hammer. You're wearing my robe.

Toni nodded. And I used your shower and I've been all through your house.

How did you wake so early?

I always wake at the same time, Toni said. I have a little alarm clock in my head.

You're so brown, Morgen said. You sleep so sweetly in your smooth brown skin, Toni.

Toni laughed. Shall I tell you a secret? It's really a suit of long brown underwear. I had it knitted on me. Would you like me to make coffee?

Yes, Morgen said, but not now.

Have you ever seen two little foxes sleeping? They sleep like this with their noses touching.

You have a sweet nose, Morgen said. She kissed it. And I love the way your hair fits your head like a little karakul cap. Let's sleep again, shall we?

Toni shook her head. I gave Isolde an egg and she thanked me so nicely and said, What's happened to Morgen, has she moved? Morgen, do you know what time it is?

It doesn't matter.

Toni's eyes lifted, went all around the room and paused. That's your mother, isn't it?

Yes.

I'm not sure, Toni said slowly, but I think the little flower she holds divided and became your eyes somehow.

Oh, Toni. Toni look at me. When I think of what I have now and what I didn't have before.

Toni bent suddenly and bit into the bend of Morgen's arm with careful teeth. There, she said, that's for thinking of what you didn't have before. She bent again and kissed the faint teethmarks. I haven't said I love you this morning. Before Morgen could move she slipped out of her arms. I'll go make coffee and then I've got to go up and see how my house is getting along without me.

Not yet, Morgen said. Don't go yet.

I'm gone, Toni said, laughing, going through the door.

Morgen turned and pushed back her hair and lay with her hands under her head and a moment of unbelieving moved in her and made her doubt the steps she heard. She looked at the sunlight in the room and she felt light and warm as sunlight and she went back to the sound of

Toni's quick light steps and the slap of the scuffs on her
bare heels and she smiled and wanted never to go beyond
this moment of light motionless pause.

When Toni came with the coffee she was wearing her
shoes and their dry stiffened soles made a clatter like
wooden shoes. She put the tray on the bed and Morgen
looked at it and laughed. Oh, I couldn't eat so early,
Toni.

Early! Toni slipped out of the robe and began swiftly
to dress. She was dressed before Morgen finished pouring
the coffee. Toni sat on the edge of the bed and buttered a
piece of roll. One looked languidly at her coffee, she said
gravely, and one ate with gusto. I'm the one eating with
gusto, she said, putting the piece of roll into her mouth.

Morgen sat holding her coffee. I can't believe you're
that one you were then.

Toni looked at her. We're neither of us the ones we
were then.

SHE lifted her head to look at Toni and, reassured,
lowered her head again. Her eyes found the tip of branch,
touched it again and swung outward toward the blue sky
and lay against it. When you're not with me, she said, I
think about it and get lost, I'm nowhere. But I've told
you now and I won't have to think about it any more,
not until he comes back. Her eyes turned against the sky
and almost closed. You've been everywhere and known so
many people, Toni, and I've been nowhere and can count
all the people I've ever known on one hand and yet —

Hello!

They looked up the hill and saw Mark coming toward
them. Morgen lifted her hand but didn't otherwise move.

His voice came ahead of him down the hill. If I ever
saw a demoralizing spectacle. One look at you two and

there went my day. He put the day on his hand and tossed it upward.

Morgen sat up.

Don't do that, he said, coming down to the wall, it spoils the picture.

Oh, I know, Morgen said, laughing. Spring fever sweeps Berkeley hills.

That's it, he said. He folded his arms on the wall and went to sleep without closing his eyes. Boy, I wish I had a boat. If I had a boat we'd all go sailing.

Morgen smiled at Toni over his head. That's what we're going to do, only not sailing.

Ferryboating, he said. That's no good.

We're going shopping, Morgen said.

On a day like this?

I was thinking about beer, Morgen said. Would you like some beer, Mark?

Sure, he said. One glass and I'll be out of my misery.

Morgen swung her feet over the wall and jumped. Come on, Toni.

Toni jumped, gathering herself together neatly.

What about me? Mark said, on the other side of the wall.

Well, Morgen said, we could bring the beer out here.

He made feeble efforts to lift himself and they stood smiling up at him and then without any preparation at all he sailed over the wall and landed just in front of them. There! He took a big breath of sunlit air. That's the last tap of work I do today.

They started across the terrace and he walked behind and looked at Toni's hair almost blue in the sun and Morgen's hair as bright as the sun itself and then his eyes picked up the V of their arms swinging easily between them but the hands held together closely and at the same time he thought of the way Morgen's eyes had measured the distance between his eyes and hers, clear and friendly but the distance there, and all the time he was walking behind them and Morgen said, I haven't looked about the beer for a long time. What if there isn't any? and then they all went in the back door.

Standing in the kitchen he looked idly at everything and said to no one, Well, I'll be damned.

Morgen knelt at the icebox door. What about? she said and looked into the compartment where she kept the beer. Oh, there's plenty. Why will you be damned, Mark?

Mark got the bottle opener out of the drawer and smiled down at her and took the bottles she handed up to him. A thing I just thought of, he said. Skip it. After that everything was just the same, except for Toni, standing small and dark against the cupboard, watching him uncap the beer and saying nothing.

He gave her a glass and she said, Thank you, and he smiled and said, That reminds me, you haven't said one word in ten minutes. You and Morgen must have been dipped in the same water. He saw their eyes, amused, touch and acknowledge and he drank off half his glass and said, That's better. If you've got anything to eat, Morgen, you'd better get ready to feed an army.

Let's see, Morgen said.

He leaned over her shoulder to look into the icebox with her. He wondered why a thing he had half known for years and dreaded knowing wholly should make him happy, seen as he was seeing it now. I could do with some of whatever's in that glass on a piece of bread, he said, if you've got any bread. He drank some more beer. He could feel them over and around him in the room and he knew it wouldn't matter a damn to them but he wished he could tell them he was happy about it.

WHEN they came out into the street they saw the day turning toward sunset with a great fanfare of traffic sounds and they stood together on the steps and Toni said softly, The world's so full of spring, Morgen. Let's not go home.

Morgen, standing a step below her, was almost as tall as she was. They smiled at this and Morgen said, I'll do anything but ride on a roller coaster.

Come on then, Toni said. She signaled the starter and he signaled a taxi and they waited at the curb and the taxi drew up and they got in. Drive ahead until I tell you where to go, Toni said. The driver nodded and Toni said, You tell him where to take us.

But, Morgen said.

Start with A then. Toni prepared to count on her fingers.

Aquarium? Morgen said. Art gallery?

Toni clasped her hand around her four fingers and leaned forward. Driver, she said, take us to the aquarium.

A moment later they were going swiftly through the street sounds outside.

TONI looked steadily into the idiotic eyes of the moray. Morgen, he looks just like the witch in Hansel and Gretel, doesn't he?

She, Morgen said.

Toni looked up and saw Morgen not looking at the moray. She straightened, laughing. Come on, she said. Where were they?

Back this way, Morgen said.

All the same, Morgen, I'd give my vote to the moray. If you'd really look at him you'd —

Here they are, Morgen said. She went close to the glass. Did you know the Little People have these for dinner on Fridays, Toni?

Confetti fish, Toni said, smiling. Yes, I've heard of it.

Morgen laughed and held Toni's arm closer. In that room windowed with shining water her laughter had a water sound. Shall we go round again?

Toni shook her head. It's after closing right now. Anyway I'd have to look at the moray again and then we'd come back here to cleanse our eyes. Come on.

Outside they walked down past the seal tanks and the seals were barking and there were still crowds of people fencing the tanks. They went on across the drive. A gardener turned into the path ahead of them. He was whistling "I Dream of Jeanie with the Light Brown Hair." At the top of the steps he turned and glanced back at them and Morgen smiled and he touched his cap to her. They went down into the concourse and when they were among the trees Toni's legs went suddenly strengthless and she dropped onto a bench. Morgen sat beside her. They were under an umbrella of branches. The last sunlight came through faintly, spattering the path.

I didn't know it till I sat down, Toni said, but I'm too tired ever to move again. I'll have to sit here and die of exposure and hunger.

Poor sweet.

I'm so young, Toni said. She touched her palm with her lips and took Morgen's hand. I'm much too young to die, Morgen.

They stood smiling at each other and then that stillness like a long pause in the heart's beating settled over them.

SHE sat on the hearth combing her almost dry hair with her fingers. Toni said, I'll be back in half an hour and if you aren't up a terrible thing will happen. Morgen thought of all the terrible things that could have happened and smiled and a knock sounded and she looked up quickly. The doorlatch clicked, but before the door opened she knew it wasn't Toni.

He saw her bright hair pouring through her fingers and he stood still in the doorway with his heart shaken and no words. He closed the door softly and went toward her.

She looked up at him, holding back her hair with both hands, and said, Why, Royal, in a faint unbelieving voice.

He sat on the hearth beside her. I didn't mean to surprise you that much, darling. He kissed the warm hand holding back her hair. Picture of old age abject before beauty, he said, smiling. Lord, I feel punch drunk. He took her hand away from her hair and held it tightly. You didn't get my wire, did you? I took the notice out of the door just now.

I must have been asleep, Morgen said. I slept late.

He tossed the notice in the fire. It doesn't matter. You're here and I'm here, if you'd just stop being amazed and see me. Oh, darling. He drew back a little to look at her. He looked at her for a long time, trying to find something in her face, some answer to what he knew was in his face. He began to feel like a clock running down.

She rose and said, Would you like some coffee? and he rose, letting his hand drop away from hers. He pulled off his muffler and the other glove and stuffed them into his coat pocket. Morgen, is something the matter?

She shook her head. No, only seeing you unexpectedly —

Aren't you well, Morgen?

Of course, she said.

He unbuttoned his coat. He wasn't going to get excited about it. Something had happened, something she couldn't tell him about. Somebody had died. Who the hell could've died? She might be pregnant. No, you wouldn't know so soon. How soon would a girl know? But she couldn't be pregnant. He got a cigarette and put it in his mouth. Well, he wasn't going to get excited about it.

Morgen said, You look so well, and then they heard the back door open and close and they turned and Toni came into the kitchen doorway, smiling at first and then not smiling, though her face didn't change at all. Hello, she said.

Royal took the cigarette out of his mouth and Morgen felt breath lift the weight out of her throat and she said, Come in, and then almost gaily she said, Toni, this is Royal.

Toni nodded to Royal and Royal, relaxing, bowed to her and said smiling, How do you do, Toni. I like first names, don't you?

Toni came across the room and stood back of the divan. They're much nicer. Her eyes went from him to Morgen with their gentle smile. You washed your hair.

Morgen nodded. It's dry, she said, touching the loose ends at the back of her neck, and breakfast's waiting.

Breakfast! Royal said. He laughed and struck a match and held his left hand out toward Morgen. Aren't you a little late?

She pushed back his cuff and looked at his watch. It was two-twenty. I don't believe it, she said, but breakfast or lunch, it's ready.

She went out into the kitchen then and Royal tossed the match toward the fireplace and inhaled and exhaled slowly, shaping the gray smoke carefully with his lips. Everything was all right now but he couldn't understand why his coming unexpectedly had knocked such a hole into her. If the girl hadn't come in they might still have been standing there like a couple of floor lamps. He glanced at the girl and found her looking at him and he smiled but said nothing and wondered who she was and where she'd been to get a tan like that and how a hairdresser ever managed to make that marvelous hair fit all over her head like a cap. Morgen came in and he turned and said, Can I help? and went toward her.

No, thank you, she said. You sit there, Royal. Toni, you sit here.

Royal put his hands flat on the table and leaned over it. Lord, does anything smell finer than a pot of fresh coffee?

Toni helped Morgen empty the tray and then Morgen went back into the kitchen and Royal breathed the warm fragrant air over the coffeepot and smiled at Toni and smiled at everything on the table and suddenly he felt lightheaded with gladness because he was back again.

When they were seated he leaned back in his chair and looked so long at Morgen out of this gladness Toni felt her heart go to her head and begin to beat softly against her temples. Funny thing, he said slowly, coming down out of winter into spring this way. Turning to Toni he said politely, I've been up in the snow and it's a marvelous business, going to sleep with the night white outside your window and waking with spring there, green hills and flowers blooming along the rights of way.

I know, Toni said. She sipped her coffee and looked down at her plate without appetite.

A month ago, Morgen said, Toni was in Switzerland.

Royal looked at Toni again. Oh, that accounts for the brown skin. You know, you two ought to hire each other for companion pieces. They looked at him and he smiled and said, You complement each other so nicely.

Morgen laughed and looked at Toni. We do, don't we? Toni and her aunt have moved into the little house above Mark's, Royal.

My house? He put down his knife and fork.

Morgen nodded. More coffee, Toni?

Yes, thanks.

My house, Royal said. Wouldn't that be my luck?

But you see, Morgen said, it belonged to Toni all the time. More coffee?

Please.

As he took back his cup it struck him that something was still terribly wrong. He didn't know how to put his finger on it but it was there. There was too much effort all the way around to keep the ball rolling. He looked at his coffee and tried to piece it together, but it was no good.

HE pushed his hands down into his pockets and turned. Morgen was leaning against the closed door, watching him with her eyes dark and too still. He knew that look but he said, That wasn't very nice of you, darling. You practically asked her to leave.

Morgen left the door. You wanted her to go.

He felt his face darken. All right, he said, but you could have done it differently.

She went to the window seat and sat down and he followed and stood in front of her. Morgen, for God's sake, what's the matter? Something's all wrong. What's happened to you?

I'll tell you, she said.

Well, let's have it.

Sit down, she said. He sat down and she looked at him for a moment with her eyes still and then she said, Before you went away, Royal, there was never any way to answer you except to say I didn't love you and you accepted that because you thought you could change it. But you should have known you can't teach a person those things, they're there or not there. I know because now I'm not alone and

I knew the moment I stopped being alone. I'm not just myself now, Royal. I'm two and the other one is Toni.

The blood went slowly out of his face and he said, Toni? and it didn't make sense at first but in the next instant it did. He remembered all the things Gildo had said and everything was perfectly clear to him, what he should have seen the moment Toni came into the room. Only it couldn't happen that way. He looked down at his hand clasped around his ankle and made himself wait. He wasn't going to say a lot of things. He let his eyes move away from his hand and then he let his foot slip off his knee to the floor and he rose and walked down the room and stopped at the table and looked at the coffee pot and the plates with food still on them and at the platter, empty except for a scrap of bacon cemented to it with cold fat. That's my heart, he thought, sliced thin, ruffled at the edges. He saw the three of them sitting there pretending to eat breakfast, a three-cornered hat, and then the whole thing hit him behind the eyes and his eyes blurred and he wanted to hit something so hard his knuckles would crack. He fitted his left hand over the knuckles of his right hand and stood trembling.

When he went back to Morgen the trembling had left him and he felt tired and empty but his voice was his own and he kept it soft and said, I don't believe it, Morgen. I won't believe it in a thousand years. Please let me talk. I don't believe it's the whole thing you think it is. It couldn't be. She's just a kid. And you've only known her a week. You don't get to know a person in a week, Morgen. I know. Morgen wasn't looking at him. He wasn't sure she was even listening but he kept his voice soft and said, I know what it is, Morgen. It's that part of your life you missed and didn't have a chance to know till you met her. But it isn't permanent, it isn't the whole thing, it couldn't be. He felt the ticker tape of words running out and he stood up and ran his hand back over his hair.

Morgen thought he had said everything he wanted to say but she wasn't sure. She waited. After a long time of silence she rose and stood beside him but he didn't turn, nothing in him turned. He was looking out down the slope of the hill. He took a breath down into his weariness finally and said, I'll go now, but he didn't move. He didn't want to go. He wanted her to talk and he wanted to batter down everything she said and show her what lay beneath it, but he knew he would go. He felt Morgen take his hand and he heard her say, Dear Royal, and he felt her face against his hand. He turned to her then and he knew for the first time what she meant when she said Dear Royal.

A few of the publications of
THE NAIAD PRESS, INC.
P.O. Box 10543 • Tallahassee, Florida 32302
Mail orders welcome. Please include 15% postage.

Spring Forward/Fall Back by Sheila Ortiz Taylor. A novel. 288 pp.
    ISBN 0-930044-70-3 $7.95

For Keeps by Elisabeth C. Nonas. A novel. 144 pp.
    ISBN 0-930044-71-1 $7.95

Torchlight to Valhalla by Gail Wilhelm. A novel. 128 pp.
    ISBN 0-930044-68-1 $7.95

Lesbian Nuns: Breaking Silence edited by Rosemary Curb and
    Nancy Manahan. Autobiographies. 432 pp.
    ISBN 0-930044-62-2 $9.95
    ISBN 0-930044-63-0 $16.95

The Swashbuckler by Lee Lynch. A novel. 288 pp.
    ISBN 0-930044-66-5 $7.95

Misfortune's Friend by Sarah Aldridge. A novel. 320 pp.
    ISBN 0-930044-67-3 $7.95

A Studio of One's Own by Ann Stokes. Edited by Dolores
    Klaich. Autobiography. 128 pp. ISBN 0-930044-64-9 $7.95

Sex Variant Women in Literature by Jeannette Howard Foster.
    Literary history. 448 pp. ISBN 0-930044-65-7 $8.95

A Hot-Eyed Moderate by Jane Rule. Essays. 252 pp.
    ISBN 0-930044-57-6 $7.95
    ISBN 0-930044-59-2 $13.95

Inland Passage and Other Stories by Jane Rule. 288 pp.
    ISBN 0-930044-56-8 $7.95
    ISBN 0-930044-58-4 $13.95

We Too Are Drifting by Gale Wilhelm. A novel. 128 pp.
    ISBN 0-930044-61-4 $6.95

Amateur City by Katherine V. Forrest. A mystery novel. 224 pp.
    ISBN 0-930044-55-X $7.95

The Sophie Horowitz Story by Sarah Schulman. A novel. 176 pp.
    ISBN 0-930044-54-1 $7.95

The Young in One Another's Arms by Jane Rule. A novel.
    224 pp. ISBN 0-930044-53-3 $7.95

The Burnton Widows by Vicki P. McConnell. A mystery novel.
    272 pp. ISBN 0-930044-52-5 $7.95

Old Dyke Tales by Lee Lynch. Short stories. 224 pp.
ISBN 0-930044-51-7 $7.95

Daughters of a Coral Dawn by Katherine V. Forrest. Science
fiction. 240 pp. ISBN 0-930044-50-9 $7.95

The Price of Salt by Claire Morgan. A novel. 288 pp.
ISBN 0-930044-49-5 $7.95

Against the Season by Jane Rule. A novel. 224 pp.
ISBN 0-930044-48-7 $7.95

Lovers in the Present Afternoon by Kathleen Fleming. A novel.
288 pp. ISBN 0-930044-46-0 $8.50

Toothpick House by Lee Lynch. A novel. 264 pp.
ISBN 0-930044-45-2 $7.95

Madame Aurora by Sarah Aldridge. A novel. 256 pp.
ISBN 0-930044-44-4 $7.95

Curious Wine by Katherine V. Forrest. A novel. 176 pp.
ISBN 0-930044-43-6 $7.50

Black Lesbian in White America by Anita Cornwell. Short stories,
essays, autobiography. 144 pp. ISBN 0-930044-41-X $7.50

Contract with the World by Jane Rule. A novel. 340 pp.
ISBN 0-930044-28-2 $7.95

Yantras of Womanlove by Tee A. Corinne. Photographs.
64 pp. ISBN 0-930044-30-4 $6.95

Mrs. Porter's Letter by Vicki P. McConnell. A mystery novel.
224 pp. ISBN 0-930044-29-0 $6.95

To the Cleveland Station by Carol Anne Douglas. A novel.
192 pp. ISBN 0-930044-27-4 $6.95

The Nesting Place by Sarah Aldridge. A novel. 224 pp.
ISBN 0-930044-26-6 $6.95

This Is Not for You by Jane Rule. A novel. 284 pp.
ISBN 0-930044-25-8 $7.95

Faultline by Sheila Ortiz Taylor. A novel. 140 pp.
ISBN 0-930044-24-X $6.95

The Lesbian in Literature by Barbara Grier. 3d ed. Foreword by
Maida Tilchen. A comprehensive bibliography. 240 pp.
ISBN 0-930044-23-1 $7.95

Anna's Country by Elizabeth Lang. A novel. 208 pp.
ISBN 0-930044-19-3 $6.95

Prism by Valerie Taylor. A novel. 158 pp.
ISBN 0-930044-18-5 $6.95

Black Lesbians: An Annotated Bibliography compiled by
J. R. Roberts. Foreword by Barbara Smith. 112 pp.
ISBN 0-930044-21-5 $5.95

The Marquise and the Novice by Victoria Ramstetter. A novel.
108 pp. ISBN 0-930044-16-9 $4.95

Labiaflowers by Tee A. Corinne. 40 pp.
ISBN 0-930044-20-7 $3.95

Outlander by Jane Rule. Short stories, essays. 207 pp.
ISBN 0-930044-17-7 $6.95

Sapphistry: The Book of Lesbian Sexuality by Pat Califia. 2nd
edition, revised. 195 pp. ISBN 0-930044-47-9 $7.95

All True Lovers by Sarah Aldridge. A novel. 292 pp.
ISBN 0-930044-10-X $6.95

A Woman Appeared to Me by Renee Vivien. Translated by
Jeannette H. Foster. A novel. xxxi, 65 pp.
ISBN 0-930044-06-1 $5.00

Cytherea's Breath by Sarah Aldridge. A novel. 240 pp.
ISBN 0-930044-02-9 $6.95

Tottie by Sarah Aldridge. A novel. 181 pp.
ISBN 0-930044-01-0 $6.95

The Latecomer by Sarah Aldridge. A novel. 107 pp.
ISBN 0-930044-00-2 $5.00

VOLUTE BOOKS

Journey to Fulfillment	by Valerie Taylor	$3.95
A World without Men	by Valerie Taylor	$3.95
Return to Lesbos	by Valerie Taylor	$3.95
Desert of the Heart	by Jane Rule	$3.95
Odd Girl Out	by Ann Bannon	$3.95
I Am a Woman	by Ann Bannon	$3.95
Women in the Shadows	by Ann Bannon	$3.95
Journey to a Woman	by Ann Bannon	$3.95
Beebo Brinker	by Ann Bannon	$3.95

These are just a few of the many Naiad Press titles. Please request a complete catalog! We encourage and welcome direct mail orders from individuals who have limited access to bookstores carrying our publications.